MW01344225

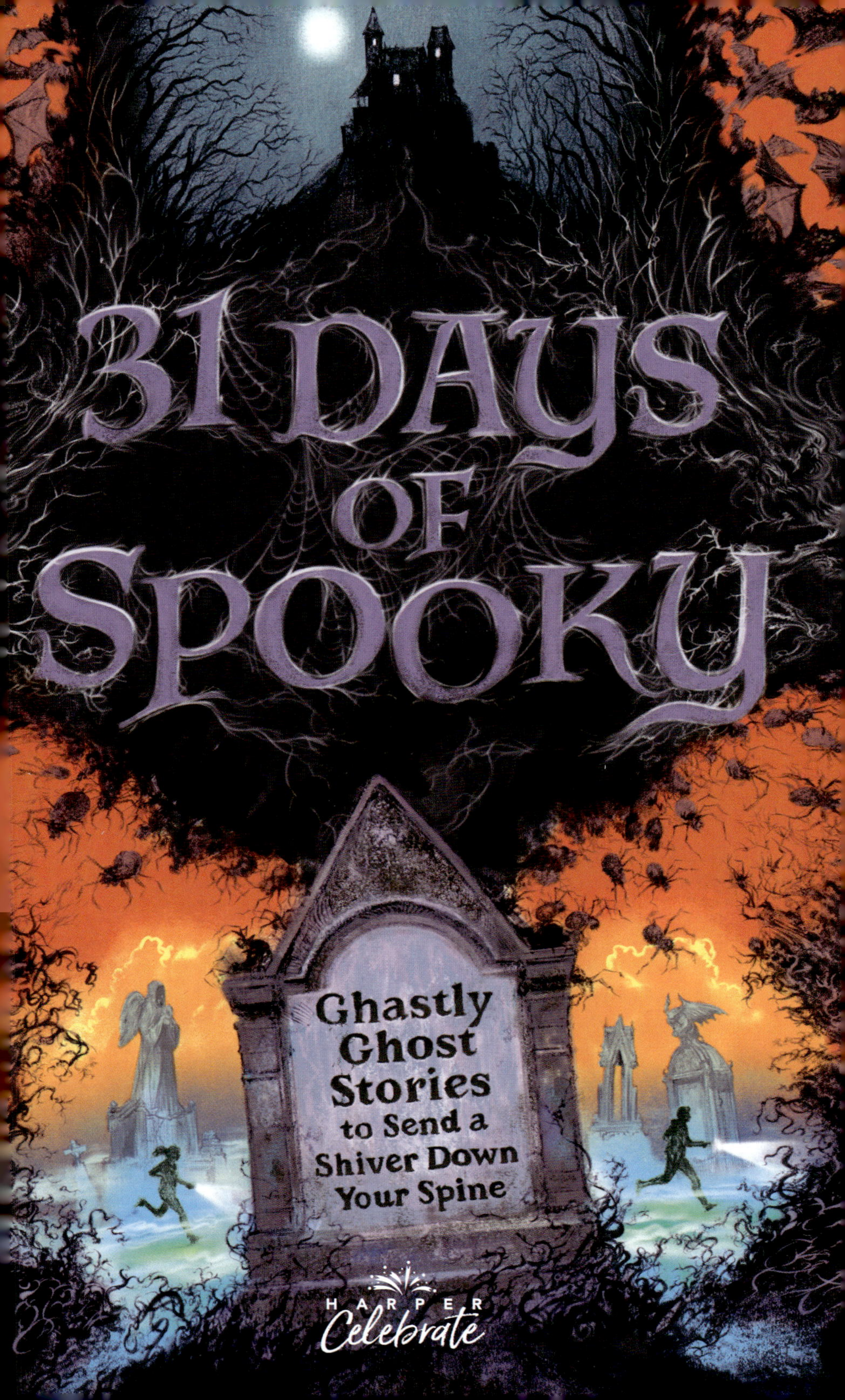
31 DAYS OF SPOOKY
Ghastly Ghost Stories to Send a Shiver Down Your Spine
HARPER Celebrate

31 Days of Spooky

Published by Harper Celebrate, an imprint of HarperCollins Focus LLC.

Cover design and interior art by Neil Evans

ISBN 978-1-4002-5241-1 (HC)
ISBN 978-1-4002-5372-2 (epub)

Printed in Malaysia

25 26 27 28 29 VPM 5 4 3 2 1

Contents

Dear reader,
If I were you,
I'd keep
the lights on.

Buried Treasure

"My guess is it's a few hundred bucks," Jared said. "A rainy-day fund that would have been worth a lot more a few decades ago than it is now."

"Maybe it's that fancy pocket watch I saw on him in all the pictures," India guessed. "I've never seen it in person."

When she was a little girl, India's mother had told stories about how she practically grew up at her grandfather's butcher shop, which was located in a local strip mall, squeezed between a sandwich shop and a bakery. Each of the three shops was owned by rival brothers—Earl, Carlos, and Bill—and they had a longstanding history of sabotaging one another's businesses. A mysterious flood, destroyed shipments, emptied cash registers—the stories had become a family legend at this point, but at the time, the family war was intense, and it bred secrecy among the family units.

For instance, India's mother told her about how her grandfather Earl supposedly kept his finest goods under a secret trapdoor in the basement of the butcher shop, and he never told anyone where it was. His ghost, India's mom said, still haunted the shop, stopping anyone from stealing his treasure.

India suspected the story was just to keep her from wandering around the dangerous equipment when she was a little girl. But now, more than two decades later, reunited for her parents' fiftieth anniversary, India and her cousin Jared were determined to get to the bottom of the family legend. They snagged the key from the junk drawer and popped over to the shop.

"I've stuck my head in once or twice, but I was always too scared to actually go in," Jared recalled. "I tended to spend my time over at the bakery."

"How do we even know what we're looking for?" India asked as she descended into the damp basement with her phone's flashlight illuminating the steps. She hadn't been in the butcher shop in over a decade, and she rarely frequented the basement. The phone's light flashed against the metal of the equipment stored down below.

"Was that a rat?" India asked as she heard an animal rustling through the shelves. The moon was full, and its light cascaded through the small window in the corner.

The smell of dried animal blood from the butchering competed with notes of sandalwood and musk, her grandfather Earl's old cologne. Rows of machines, aprons, and large brown bags filled the space. Quarters were cramped between the two of them.

"Just start opening stuff, I guess," Jared said.

India lifted one of the giant brown bags, and suddenly, a dim, green fluorescent bulb flickered to life above her.

Both India and Jared jumped, surprised by the sudden light. They heard a howl from outside the shop.

"Did you turn that on?" Jared looked cautiously at the lantern. India shook her head.

Jared turned pale and wondered aloud if they should leave, but India was determined to see it through.

"This shouldn't take us long. It's not like there's a lot of ground to cover," she insisted.

That's when she noticed a sand-speckled tarp covering a bottom shelf, and she leaned down to inspect where its corner met the wall.

"I would guess we're looking for a hole." India lifted the corner of the tarp.

The green light turned back off. Jared dropped the box he'd been inspecting. India turned her phone's flashlight on, excited by the adventure.

Sure enough, in the back left corner, hidden by the tarp, there was an old plank of wood covering a hole in the floor.

"X marks the spot," India joked.

When she touched the wood plank, the green light began flickering in rapid succession.

On.

Off.

On.

Off.

The door to the basement clanged shut, startling them both.

"Is this a good idea?" Jared asked as India moved the plank aside.

"Seems like Grandpa Earl knows we're close to finding it." India acted as if she were joking, but she was secretly spooked out.

India hesitated, and Jared leaned forward.

"What is it?" Jared said.

Inside the shallow hole was a single object wrapped in a piece of cloth. She picked it up.

Afraid of how Earl's ghost would react—if it even existed—India carefully lifted the object out and unwrapped a worn leather bifold wallet. Opening it, she saw a sallow, yellow piece of paper featuring a list of names.

A fearsome sound, like a coyote howling, filled the night as a creature dashed across the window.

"Put it back!" Jared demanded, a tremor in his voice.

"His treasure," India whispered, showing the list to Jared.

His eyes were darting between the closed door and the still-flashing light.

"We have to get out of here." Jared grabbed the list from India's hand and started to wrap it back up in the wallet. But then he stopped and gasped. "Look."

India stared at the list in the flickering light. Most of the names on the list had been crossed out, but there was Jared's father's name—Robert—one of two remaining names, written clear as day. India scanned the names that had been crossed

out, recalling how she'd attended all of their funerals over the last decade.

India and Jared stared at one another.

"Do you think . . . ?" India was horrified at the thought. She looked around at the giant knives hanging around the ceiling. "Surely not." Grandpa Earl had always been so sweet.

"I have to warn Dad." Jared frantically pulled out his phone, but they had no service down in the basement. "It's dead!" he exclaimed as he rushed back up the stairs.

The green light turned on, almost blinding them now as they escaped the shop.

Jared drove wildly, blasting through every stop sign and red light, weaving around traffic in the pouring rain.

As they neared the house, Jared swerved to miss a coyote standing in the middle of the road. India noticed the moonlight produced an increasingly greenish cast.

"Stop!" India yelled when she saw a silhouette of a man walking in slow motion down the center of the road.

"Dad!" Jared yelled, jumping from the car.

Robert awoke from his trance, a small bottle of sandalwood and musk in his hand.

"What are you doing?" Jared pleaded.

"I . . . I don't know . . . ," he stammered. "But Earl asked me to bring this to him."

Down with the Ship

Rain pelted the deck of the boat, and a thick mist rolled in. The storm had closed in fast. If Jim had known the bad weather was coming, he would've told the crew to steer the boat back to shore early.

Too late now, he thought, shaking his head. *Best we can do is wait it out.*

Two of the crewmen were up at the wheel, arguing over how long the rain would last. The other two crewmen were at the side of the boat, securing the salmon fishing nets they had been pulling in before the rain started.

"Need a hand?" Jim asked as he walked over to the men working on the nets.

"Could use one, Captain," Dale answered, continuing to work. "Waves got the lines tangled up."

Jim got to work helping haul in the nets. All three men were drenched from the rain, but they were used to the wet conditions.

"Are you seeing this?" Jim asked, gazing at the horizon.

"Seeing what?" Dale said as he scanned across the bay. "The waters look choppy, but nothing out of the usual."

"That huge ship. It looks like it's heading straight toward us."

Running for the wheel, Jim shouted out orders to the crewmen. He sent Dale to bring up the anchor, just in case they needed to move. Even though the approaching ship should give them the right of way, he had seen plenty of rule-breaking captains when the conditions were bad. Better safe than sorry.

Jim sounded the horn, thinking maybe the ship hadn't seen them. But the ship didn't change course, and no sound answered. He hit the horn a second time. The rest of the crew darted around quickly, surreptitiously looking at one another. No one else knew what Jim was seeing, but out of respect, they didn't doubt their captain.

The ship kept coming, undeterred by the boat directly in its path. Desperately, Jim turned the wheel of his fishing boat, jolting the crew as he changed course.

One of the nets they had worked so hard to secure went sailing over the side of the boat, splashing into the water below. Scrambling, Dale reached for it, hoisting in the heavy, soaked rope, and the rest of the crew rushed over to help him drag it in while Jim tried his best to steady the reeling boat.

As they struggled, the oncoming ship sailed past, plowing right through the spot they had been in moments before. Water crashed onto the deck, rocking the boat to and fro. Enraged, Jim caught sight of the ship's name on the bow.

"What was that?" Dale shouted, soaked head to toe.

Jim could barely make out the name painted on the side.

"*The Lady Grace*," he stated.

After the storm passed, the crew successfully docked the ship, still perplexed at Jim's visions and what had actually caused the disturbance in the water. Meanwhile, Jim made his way to the coast guard's office.

"I'd like to report a vessel," Jim said to the young man behind the desk.

""'Kay," the man replied with a sigh, obviously annoyed at the prospect of paperwork.

"A ship nearly hit my fishing boat during the storm today," Jim explained. "It didn't even seem to notice we were there. Would have run right into us if I hadn't swerved." Jim noticed the man's gaze had dropped down to his papers. Jim banged on the counter. "Did you catch that? I'm sorry, I didn't get your name."

"Marc."

"Marc, are you taking this down? This captain shouldn't have a license. We could have died."

"Did you get the name of the ship?" Marc still hadn't so much as picked up a pen to start the report.

"Saw the name on the bow," Jim replied. "*The Lady Grace*."

"*The Lady Grace*?" Marc blinked at Jim.

"Yes, that's definitely what it said."

Marc chuckled and leaned back in his seat.

Angered, Jim asked, "What's so funny?"

"*The Lady Grace* crashed into some rocks off the coast twenty years ago. The crew had to abandon it after a storm. Rumor is the captain's wife, Grace, died on those very same rocks, pulled out to sea while she was waiting for him to return one fateful evening. Then, just a few months later, the captain lost his life on those same rocks. To this day, there are tales of the ghost ship sailing these waters. I haven't talked to anyone else who actually set eyes on it though. They say . . ." His voice faded.

"They say what?" Jim pressed.

"Only the heartbroken can see it," Marc mumbled.

Jim swallowed, perturbed at this insolent kid. Who put him up to this?

"I know what I saw," Jim pushed.

"More rain's coming in. I suggest you get on home to your sweetie if you got one."

"I don't," Jim responded bluntly.

"Oh." Marc blushed. "Well, either way, time to be going home before these storms set in again. They're a doozy."

Jim drove home, huge drops of rain splashing on his windshield. He entered his house soaked and grabbed a cheap bottle of wine from the cabinet.

He and his wife, Elena, always saved the nice bottles for special occasions. Jim couldn't think of any special occasions ever again, not without her, and so the good bottles collected layer upon layer of dust while he kept replacing the cheap ones more often than he'd like to admit. He selected a five-buck bottle and sank aimlessly into the couch under the unrelenting patter of the rain on his tin roof.

The weather the next day was drastically clearer, with blue skies and a shining sun. Jim's mood, however, was anything but sunny. It had been another long, sleepless night. If he was honest, he hadn't slept well since he lost Elena out at sea nine months ago.

But his crew needed him. They pushed out from the dock and got to work.

After a few hours out on the water, Jim saw the shadow of a ship on the horizon. He recognized the shape of it, and a pit formed in his stomach. *Not again.*

He looked at his crew. No one else seemed to have noticed, even as the ship inched closer and closer to their boat. Jim tried his best to remain calm.

Standing behind the wheel were two shadowy figures in the fog. Jim swore he could see straight through them. He blinked and looked closer. Surely the light was playing tricks on him. They were laughing, steering, drinking wine—surely it was the captain and Grace, two lovers reunited in death, toasting together in a perpetual celebration.

They turned and lifted their glasses toward Jim, and he saluted them in return. Ghosts or not, he couldn't be sure, but he couldn't help but marvel at their happiness.

As he was staring at them, a third shadowy figure emerged from the back of *The Lady Grace*. A chill ran through Jim's body. He knew that silhouette, the tilt of her head, the cascade of her hair. The salt air turned to scents of lavender.

Elena lifted a hand in a solemn wave.

"I'm coming for you," Jim whispered in a tone so low no other human could hear.

Her voice echoed in his ears.

"Don't hurry. There's plenty of time." She always had been the patient one.

"I don't want to live in a time without you in it," he whispered, tears rolling down his face. Everything else fell from his sight. All he could see was her, his beloved wife.

"I'll always be here, sailing on the horizon, just as we've always done," Elena replied. He started to object, but she interrupted. "Don't worry about me, I mean it. And, Jim?"

"Yes?"

"When you get here, we'll drink the good stuff, okay?"

"Okay." He chuckled.

And with that she dissipated into the fog. Jim wiped his eyes as the smell of salt returned.

He dropped his head and went back to work. The crew was shocked by the depth of focus and determination he had. It seemed, maybe, the old Jim was back.

That night, when Jim arrived home, his face still salty from the wind and tears, he went to his cabinet. He impulsively reached for one of the cheap bottles, but he stopped himself. As he leaned down to lift one of the dusty bottles from the bottom shelf, he swore he could smell lavender. He wiped away the dust and a large, goofy smile spread across his face when he read the label.

The Lady Grace.

Jim poured two glasses, toasted the air, and finally drank the good stuff.

Summer Party

Margaret had always thought the big old house in the Massachusetts countryside was a bit stuffy in the springtime. She had visited here on several occasions to see her friend Helen—often to attend the elaborate parties that Helen would throw in the summers—but never for more than a few days at a time. This time Margaret planned to stay for at least a few weeks. Longer if Helen needed her.

Helen's son, Bobby, had been killed abroad at war, and Margaret knew Helen would need support. But as they sat in the sunroom sipping iced tea, Helen wasn't nearly as distraught as Margaret had anticipated. In fact, Helen was downright chatty.

Everyone grieves in their own way, Margaret thought, so she tried her best not to judge.

She wished there was a breeze coming through the open window to add some life into the room, the air stale and stagnant.

"I was thinking, with summer right around the corner, it's time to start planning a party," Helen said with a smile.

Margaret nearly choked on her tea. "I doubt anyone would be upset if you took this summer off from hosting."

Helen looked shocked at the idea. "Well, of course I plan to host. Everyone loves my parties."

"Given the circumstances, I think our friends would understand," Margaret said slowly.

Helen seemed a bit confused and smoothed the skirt of her blue dress. Margaret had expected to see her in mourning black, but her friend had donned bright colors.

Everyone grieves differently.

Not wanting to upset her, Margaret backtracked. "I think a summer party would be lovely."

Helen smiled, then sat back in her chair, sipping her tea.

"We should paint our nails," Helen said. "A bright pink. It's springtime, after all."

Margaret reluctantly agreed to Helen's suggestion, still perplexed by her behavior.

That night Margaret tried her best to settle into bed. The spring night had a sharp chill, so she snuggled under the thick quilt.

Just as she was falling asleep, she heard the creak of footsteps on the floorboard in the hall. Worried Helen was awake and pacing, she got up, put on a robe and slippers, and stepped out into the hall to check on her friend.

No one was there. No light in the hallway. And the sound of footsteps was gone.

Margaret got back into bed and drifted off to sleep.

Over the next few days, Margaret and Helen enjoyed salads on the porch and talked of parties. All the while, Helen smiled, laughed, and wore coastal, preppy clothes. She never mentioned Bobby.

At night, the sound of footsteps continued, rousing Margaret from her bed. But there was never anyone in the hall.

Margaret decided to bring it up one day to Helen while they were out strolling around the neighborhood, observing all the beautiful homes with wraparound porches.

"I feel like I must be going a bit mad," Margaret admitted. "Perhaps it's a housekeeper? But I never see anyone. Have you heard those sounds?"

Helen broke into an enormous grin. "Of course I have. It's Bobby."

Margaret lost her footing, nearly landing on the ground at the casual way Helen made this statement.

"I don't think I understand," Margaret said, her curiosity piqued. "You think the footsteps in the hall are . . . Bobby?"

"Yes, he keeps me company at night." Helen smiled again, clearly undisturbed by the turn the conversation had taken.

"Helen." Margaret tried to keep her voice soft, soothing. "Bobby is gone. He isn't walking the halls at night."

Helen waved a hand. "Oh, I know he's dead, but his spirit never left the house. I feel him all the time. Don't you?"

Convinced Helen was using the idea of Bobby's lingering ghost to comfort herself, Margaret agreed.

That night when she heard the footsteps, she went farther into the hall than she had before. Off in the distance, the footsteps continued lightly, treading down toward the kitchen. Margaret followed, taking a candle with her and keeping a good distance behind.

When she reached the kitchen, the sounds were gone. Looking around, she noticed the door to the basement was slightly ajar.

Sure she would catch a wandering maid, she took a few steps down the basement stairs, leaving the door open behind her.

She shivered at the sudden chill in the air. The door slammed shut, sealing out any lingering light from the kitchen. Unnerved, she turned and grabbed the door handle.

It wouldn't budge.

Tugging harder, she tried to yank the door open, but it stayed put. Locked.

Fighting the urge to hyperventilate, she turned back toward the stairs and heard the scuff of what sounded like feet shuffling ahead.

She called out a hello into the dark chasm of the basement, but nobody responded.

Margaret felt frozen in place. With the door locked behind her, there was no getting out that way. She knew there were other entrances to the basement, and she had even seen a gardener go through a door from the yard. She just had to find one of them. In the dark.

She took one tentative step down. Then another.

The noise in the basement had subsided completely, leaving Margaret with nothing but the sound of her own footsteps.

As she finished the descent, her eyes adjusted to the light of the candle. Under the stairs was a nondescript door tucked away as if it wanted to remain unnoticed.

She pushed open the hidden door carefully, surprised to find it unlocked. The smell of decay hit her immediately.

Inside the room were two wooden coffins.

She guessed before she even looked that Bobby was inside the first coffin.

It was the second coffin that surprised her. From the looks of it, the body inside had been there for weeks—at least. Despite the horrific sight of the decomposing corpse, the blue dress was unmistakable.

The second coffin held Helen's body.

Scrambling, she turned to leave, but her path was blocked by a third coffin. As it creaked open, she saw a limp hand, still flush with blood, its pink fingernails protruding from the edge. She screamed, but there was no one to hear her.

As the coffin opened, she saw her own slack-jawed face, her sagging skin, and sockets where her eyes had been.

"Come on, Margaret, let's have another salad, shall we?"

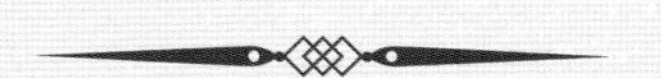

High Score

The run-down mall wasn't nearly as popular as it used to be. Brad had been working security there for over thirty years now, and he remembered the days when it was a hot spot of activity. *Not anymore*, he thought.

Mall management had put security cameras pretty much everywhere, and the security staff had dwindled from a dozen overnight team members to just one. Brad didn't mind watching the cameras by himself, but he did miss the company.

Nowadays, the little arcade at the back of the mall, with its incessantly blinking lights, was the most entertaining thing to keep an eye on.

Pinball had always been Brad's favorite game. When he had nothing better to do, which was often, he would come in early and fight for the high score. He never could seem to hold on to it for more than a few days at a time, but the pursuit always entertained him anyway.

His manager had recently started to ask Brad about when he would retire, but he had been brushing off the question. It seemed impossible to imagine what else he would do with his time. Working nights suited him just fine.

Lately, though, Brad had started to wonder if maybe his manager had a small point. Maybe he needed some time off. For the past week, when he looked at the cameras in the arcade, Brad could swear he saw an elderly man in a baseball cap walking around long after all the other workers had left.

The first night he had barged down the hall and through the arcade door, ready to arrest the perpetrator, but he hadn't found anyone inside. And when he returned to the security cameras, all looked well.

It had continued happening the past few nights, with the old man walking up to the pinball machine, playing a game on it, and then quickly disappearing. Even more odd, the date and time on the video were malfunctioning.

On one particularly quiet night, Brad hunkered down in the security booth to keep an extra-close watch on the cameras. Tonight, he was ready and waiting, prepared to record the minute the old man appeared on screen. The date in the corner of the video showed tomorrow night's date.

Brad spun around the faded Red Sox hat he wore every day, moving the brim out of the way so he could get a good view.

Sure enough, a little after midnight, a figure appeared on the screen.

"Oh, I've gotcha this time," Brad mumbled to himself as he hit Record and inched closer to the screen.

The figure of the old man was shadowy as it made its way to the pinball machine. Lights whirred and the ball flew as the old man played.

The pinball machine rang out, "High score!"

The machine flashed as the old man put his initials in the winner's spot: *BRJ*.

Funny, Brad thought. He adjusted his glasses.

The old man snuck out as soon as the pinball machine quieted. Brad didn't know how he had slipped out without him noticing. When Brad stopped the recording, he set it back to the beginning and watched it through.

There it was, plain as day.

"Finally," Brad said to himself gleefully. "I've got proof now."

He watched the video through one more time. This time he noticed that the man had turned his head slightly toward the security camera before he left, and Brad could see the clear image on the screen of a faded, well-loved Red Sox hat.

Brad saved the recording to a USB, emailed a copy to himself, and uploaded it to online storage for good measure.

The next night Brad got to work early, eager to show the video to his coworkers before they left for the evening.

"You've got to see this," Brad said, pulling an extra chair up to the computer and waving Tony over.

Brad plugged the USB into the computer and opened up the folder, but there was no video saved on it. Annoyed, he opened up his online storage. Nothing there either.

158800
HIGH BJR SCORE

“I think the night shift is getting to you.” Tony laughed, patting Brad on the shoulder. “Starting to see things. If you want to switch shifts next week, let me know.”

Tony clocked out, but Brad ignored him, pulling up his email. This was exactly why he had made sure to save the video in so many spots. But there were no emails with the video link in his inbox. Nothing in his outbox. No drafts. The video was nowhere to be found.

Frustrated, he walked down to the arcade, hoping the intruder would be there. He examined the pinball machine in question, looking around to see if anyone was in the hallway. *The only way to lure the man out,* he thought, *is to beat him at his own game.* Hopefully he wouldn’t be able to resist a challenge. Brad had achieved the high score before. Surely he could do it again and finally catch this trespasser.

As soon as he touched the machine, he felt a sharp shock, and a jolt of electricity ran through him. But still, Brad continued to play.

“High score!” the machine rang out in record time, and Brad’s ghost entered his initials. *BRJ.* He looked over his shoulder at the security camera and smiled. He’d never lose his high score again.

Late Checkout

"Checking in?"

"Yes." Meredith hoisted the duffel bag higher on her shoulder. Why had she packed so much? "Meredith Gregory."

"Welcome, Ms. Gregory, let me pull up the reservation." The front desk worker gave her a welcoming smile. She looked like she could be about Meredith's mother's age, with a name tag identifying her as Joan.

"I have you here for four nights," Joan said, clicking and typing away. "You'll be in room 306, floor three. Breakfast starts at seven and goes until ten."

Joan continued to rattle off details.

"I should warn you," Joan said seriously, catching Meredith's attention again. "Some guests say that room is haunted."

Of course it is, Meredith thought. *Small-town B and Bs always have a ghost or two.* She probably would have chosen a bigger hotel a town or two away, but her mother had insisted on staying at this bed-and-breakfast. It was tradition, she had said, since both Meredith's uncle and her mother had worked at the B and B when they were in college.

It was her mother, really, who had wanted to go on this trip. Uncle Wes was running for governor, and her mother had insisted they come on the campaign trail and support him. Meredith couldn't say she was all that excited about the trip. Uncle Wes had always frustrated her with his long-winded, know-it-all, unsolicited speeches over dinner, but she tried her best to play nice.

Still, that didn't mean she was looking forward to watching him spend the next few days hamming it up in the hopes of winning.

The room Meredith was staying in was lovely, with a large, plush bed, a cozy reading area, and even a small balcony. She opened up the balcony door, luxuriating in the fresh air while she read her book on the bed.

It was so comfortable that she dozed off, and when she woke up, she thought for a second that there was someone standing on the balcony. It must have been the unexpected nap fogging her brain because she blinked a few times and realized there was nothing there but the curtains blowing in the wind.

A knock on her door sent her bolting upright. She opened it to find her mother waiting expectantly.

"Don't tell me you're not ready," her mother lectured. "We're supposed to leave for dinner in twenty minutes!"

Meredith looked at her watch, surprised that two full hours had passed. She closed the door on her mother, promising to meet her in the lobby on time.

The dinner was long, dull, and pretentious, with her uncle regaling Meredith and her mother with stories about how much the town adored him. At least the wine was good.

Uncle Wes forced a campaign button on Meredith before she departed, which she dutifully chucked into her purse. "Wes for Governor," it read, followed by his slogan: "Winners never look back." *How typically presumptuous,* Meredith thought, *that he'd already call himself a winner when he's never even organized a neighborhood block party, much less an entire state!*

That night Meredith awoke to the sound of a door banging, and she blearily looked around. The room was pitch-black, and the balcony door was wide open, swaying in the wind.

Must not have locked it, she thought.

But then she saw it, the unmistakable shape of a woman wildly dumping the contents of Meredith's purse, the items scattering around the room. She had unruly curly hair, her feet were bare, and she was wearing a bathrobe.

Stifling a scream, Meredith held her breath as she watched the woman dash to the balcony door, clutching something shiny in her bony fingers. Then she jerked back around and locked her sad, sallow yellow eyes straight on Meredith. Meredith tried to move, but she found herself glued to her pillow under the force of the ghost's gaze.

The specter's jaw fell open as if trying to form words, but all she could muster was a high-pitched scream before she vanished.

Meredith got out of bed and put everything she could find back into her purse. Then she paced back and forth for the remaining hours, trying to comprehend what she had just seen.

The next morning she marched down to the front desk to question Joan about the ghost.

"Her name is Louisa," Joan informed her. "I'm sorry to say she died here. She jumped from the balcony when she was a guest. Must've been 1982, if I remember correctly. I was working in housekeeping back then."

Joan leaned in, dropping her voice to a whisper. "Some said she was pushed, but nobody could ever prove it."

The story lingered in Meredith's mind all day, and she found herself dwelling on it while she ate lunch at her uncle's house.

"Do you remember a woman named Louisa who worked at the hotel back in the day?" Meredith asked as her uncle slurped up the last bite of his soup.

"Never heard of her," Uncle Wes responded, glancing down the table at her mother. "Pass the bread, would you?"

Meredith tried to drop the subject, but her curiosity got the best of her. "They say she died. Some say she jumped, but others say she was murdered."

"Don't know anything about that."

"I only ask because last night . . ." Her voice trailed off. "It's silly, but I think I saw her ghost. The front desk confirmed others have seen her too."

"Interesting." Wes's blue, beady eyes pierced through her, and she felt the same paralyzed feeling she experienced the night before.

"It was like she was looking for something. Or maybe trying to tell me something. Something important," she managed to say.

Wes flashed his winning white smile.

"Sounds like some great marketing to me," he quipped. "That story will attract visitors for sure."

Uncomfortable with her uncle's dismissal, Meredith quickly finished her meal as he fed her canned campaign lines. When she left, in typical fashion, her uncle forced a dozen flyers on her and insisted she put on a campaign button.

"Wes for Governor." Meredith forced a smile as she pinned it on.

"'Winners never look back.' Remember that, Mer." He winked.

When she returned to the hotel, Joan was still at the desk. "Now there's a name I haven't seen in a while." She raised an eyebrow. "Do you know Wes?"

Meredith nodded. "He's my uncle. He used to work here, actually."

"Oh, I remember. Used to be quite the ladies' man. He talked the ear off every girl who checked in, and half the staff too. Never did take the hint."

"It's funny," Meredith said, "I asked him about Louisa, and he said he didn't remember her."

"That certainly is odd." Joan's face turned cold and hard. "Wes is the one who found her."

Meredith's mind was still reeling as she got ready for bed that night, but it wasn't long before her face-cream ritual was interrupted by a loud bang. The windows in her hotel room flew open with harsh, straight-line winds. Meredith bolted from the bathroom to find Louisa's ghost crouched like a gargoyle over the stack of campaign flyers Meredith had left on the desk. Even in the dark, it was clear in her sallow eyes that she was enraged. She let out a scream, her hair blowing wildly in all directions.

"It's okay. It's okay," Meredith whispered as if trying to tame a wild animal.

Louisa ripped the papers to shreds and threw the pieces around the room.

"Did you know him? Wes Whitehead? The man on these flyers?"

Louisa lurched toward to the balcony door, leaning her bony skeleton over the edge. But then all of a sudden, she jolted around, looking past Meredith.

"Killer!" Louisa shouted.

Meredith started to turn around, but before she could, she felt two gloved hands grip her around the neck.

Louisa's ghost screeched and slammed into the walls, smashing every object she could find, trying to alert anyone to come—anyone at all. But she was too late.

The thud of Meredith's body crashing three stories below echoed throughout the bed-and-breakfast.

Louisa's ghost threw herself after Meredith and then vanished. The wind stopped, and there was quiet.

"I warned you," croaked a smooth, confident voice. "Winners never look back."

WINNERS
NEVER
OOK BACK

The Closed Carousel

The busy summer season was finally over, which meant that Omar could close up the amusement park an hour earlier now. He loved this time of year when the rush finally died down. Summer meant long lines, people complaining about the heat, and late hours. But once fall came, the place cleared out as the sun went down.

Omar had been working in the kids' area all week, which was especially quiet now that school was back in session. Even with the reduced hours, there wasn't a lot to do.

"Hey, Omar," the lead mechanic called as he walked over. Andrew had been working at the park a lot longer than Omar, and he knew every ride like the back of his hand. "The carousel is closed for maintenance."

"Copy that," Omar responded. "Will it be up and running tomorrow, or should I let the weekend manager know it'll be closed?"

"It'll be fine by the morning." Andrew wiped grease on his overalls. "Does this every year around the beginning of fall. If it starts acting strange, just ignore it."

"If you say so," Omar said. "Hey, are you okay?" he asked, noticing a wide, garish slash on Andrew's arm.

Andrew seemed tired and kept looking over his shoulder toward the carousel. Realizing that Omar had seen the wound, he pulled the fabric of his sleeve down. "I'm fine. Clocking out and going to eat. You should head out soon yourself."

The park's official closing time came and went, and security was busy ushering out any lingering guests. Omar thought he heard the sounds of laughter nearby and did a quick sweep of the area to make sure everyone had moved toward the exit. Once the kids' area was clear, he started the process of closing up for the night.

He was the only worker assigned to this area. He had been promoted to weekday manager last summer, a new title he was very proud of.

Some of the rides in the kiddie area hadn't been used today, but the carousel was always by far the most popular. There were sure to be a few complaining parents tomorrow if Andrew was wrong about it reopening in the morning.

Most of the rides had their own lights and music, and the combination of sounds could be overwhelming at night. As he pulled the lever shutting off the last ride, Omar paused, enjoying the silence.

It won't be long now before we completely close for the winter season, Omar thought as he packed up. *Just a few weeks to go.* He had another job for the winter, but it wasn't nearly as fun as working at the park.

Just as he was getting ready to leave, Omar heard the whirring sound of gears turning, a surefire sign one of the rides wasn't fully shut down. He could have sworn they were all set for the night. Annoyed at himself, he walked around the area, confirming all the equipment was turned off.

When he got to the carousel, he paused. The control board looked like it was powered down, but the whirring noise was definitely coming from this ride.

Andrew had said it might act strange, he reminded himself.

As he examined the controls, the lights of the carousel blinked on, blinding as they cut through the dark night. The music started up, sounding far too loud as it broke the silence.

Something is definitely malfunctioning, Omar thought as he stepped back. *Probably best to let Andrew deal with it tomorrow.*

Then the carousel started moving. It was slow at first, then it picked up speed, moving faster than it normally went. The horses bobbed up and down much too quickly, and the lights flashing and music playing picked up in tempo.

Nervous, Omar looked down at the controls, worried he had flipped some switch. But everything indicated the carousel should still be off.

When he looked up again, he noticed that one of the horses appeared as if it had a rider on it. The figure seemed to be a young boy, but the carousel was going so fast that it was hard to tell. If a kid had managed to sneak on . . . Omar hated to think of what might happen to the kid.

Omar grabbed his phone and called Andrew to ask him what to do, but Andrew's phone went straight to voicemail. Omar left a frantic message, hoping Andrew would come to his aid.

The sound of a child laughing swelled all around him and over the ride's music. Omar shouted at the boy to hold on and pressed buttons on the control panel furiously, begging the carousel to stop. He had to get it to stop.

Out of nowhere, the lights went out and the music suddenly ended. The carousel jolted to an abrupt halt. Sprinting, Omar circled the carousel, checking each horse for any sign of the child. Finding nothing, he looked around the area, but there were no children.

The carousel is closed. . . . If it starts acting strange, just ignore it, Andrew had said. *Does this every year around the beginning of fall.*

The lights and music of the carousel started up again, and as it began turning in circles, Omar heard the sound of a child's laughter. It sounded like it was coming from atop one of the horses, but he didn't see any riders. His phone buzzed in his pocket. It was a text from Andrew.

Trust me. Get out now.

Taking Andrew's advice, he bolted to the exit, shaking as he went and covering his ears, the sounds of the carousel blaring behind him.

The Haunted Heist

If all went according to plan, Elsie was going to be filthy, stinking rich after this job. She had heard whispers of the Butterfly Diamond, a diamond so pure and thin it had been deemed priceless. It was like looking through a butterfly's wing, according to the cheesy brochure she had picked up from the museum while she was casing it the night before.

The diamond was on loan from some private collection, available for viewing for just a few weeks before it was locked inside a vault again for a decade or two. Then it would make the rounds again to museums, drumming up public interest and donors.

Elsie knew if she could steal the diamond and sell it, she would be set for life. Maybe she would go live somewhere tropical and sip piña coladas on a beach.

Security on a diamond this valuable is laughably light, Elsie thought as she ran through the plan again. She'd scoped out the area for the last few days, planning her heist and sorting through every unlucky situation she could imagine. There weren't even any security cameras in the room where the diamond was displayed. It was like they didn't care if anyone tried to take it.

She had timed her entrance just as the security guards were changing shifts several hours after the museum had closed, ducking under the ticket turnstile while the two guards made pointless small talk. Once she was inside, she stuck to the route she had mapped out. It was winding and took nearly three times as long as it would have if she'd walked straight there, but Elsie knew this path would keep her from passing any security patrols.

The room was dark when she slipped through the doorway with just a small light glowing beneath the diamond. It was in a glass case, but there were no alarms.

The way the light made the diamond glow was intoxicating, drawing Elsie in. The stone was spectacular, sparkling in every direction.

Elsie felt pulled to it. Called by it. It was like the diamond wanted her to take it. She couldn't imagine why nobody had ever attempted to steal it.

She approached the glass case, listening for any sounds of approaching guards. Not hearing any sounds, she took a small rubber mallet and an iron pin out of the tool pack at her hip.

With one quick crack of the mallet against the pin, the glass shattered, falling like rain around the diamond. Elsie reached out a hand, fingers covered by black gloves.

With the diamond exposed, its pull was even more intense. Elsie could have sworn she felt the air around it pulsing as her fingers inched closer.

Take me, the diamond seemed to say.

Some small, tiny voice in the back of Elsie's head sounded an alarm. This was all too easy. Why would a treasure like this be so unprotected?

She thought she heard a voice whisper behind her, and she looked around to make sure she was alone. No guards, nobody approaching, but she heard another whisper, a different voice this time.

"Don't touch it."

But Elsie wasn't sure she could ignore the call of the diamond. Now that she had seen it, now that she was so close to holding it, she was consumed by greed. She had to have it.

Unable to fight the allure of the diamond, she reached out, brushing her fingers against its smooth, glittering surface.

She felt a jerk as if she were being pulled out of her body and sucked straight into the diamond itself. It was like a vacuum, drawing her whole soul in and spitting it back out.

She blinked, and suddenly she realized she wasn't alone. There were at least a dozen other people standing around the diamond display. Most were dressed in black, like her, and some looked like their outfits were at least a century old.

Elsie scanned the faces that were all staring at her.

"It's un-stealable," one of the people said, an older man with a thick beard and a hood pulled over his head. "You should have listened. You should have left."

Confused, Elsie looked around at the people. All of them were shimmering, as if they were only half in this world. When she glanced down, she realized her hands were the same. Transparent. Like a ghost.

When she saw what lay on the floor, Elsie gasped.

Her body was crumpled on the ground, curled in on itself as though in agony.

After a few long moments, she heard a guard come down the hallway. He found her body there and called the police. Medical personnel with a stretcher came and took her corpse away. Elsie tried to follow them but was unable to.

No matter how hard she tried, she couldn't seem to make herself move more than a few feet away from the diamond. She realized the spirits were other failed thieves who had felt its call and been pulled in like flies to a trap.

"What do I do now?" Elsie asked, still trying desperately to make it more than a few steps away from the diamond. But every time, it tugged her back as if she were connected to it by a leash.

"Nothing," the bearded man said sadly. "The diamond has you now. You're one of us."

"One of you? What do you do?"

"Regret."

Family Ties

Don't run!" Lin called after Willow, who was bolting away from the tour group toward whatever her six-year-old imagination had found more exciting.

"I've got her," his wife, Eliza, said. She broke away from the group, following Willow as she skipped ahead. Her paper doll trailed behind her in the breeze.

"Honey, you lost Gabriela!" Eliza yelled as she picked up the paper doll. They had just decorated it together at the previous exhibit on the tour, and Willow had quickly grown attached to it.

The whole visit had been inspired by Willow. Her first-grade class was doing a project this month on family trees, so she had come to Lin asking about her grandparents, their parents, and so on. That was how Lin had learned his great-grandfather had been stationed at this fort when he died. Coming for a tour had seemed like a great way to learn a little more about their family history.

Lin listened carefully to what the tour guide was saying about the old military fort. The chipper guide couldn't have been more than twenty and regaled the group with grandiose stories about centuries-old battles that had been fought at the fort before it was shut down in the sixties.

As the tour guide talked and took them through the old barracks and mess hall, Lin looked at every sign and plaque, checking for his great-grandfather's name.

Willow had thought the visit was a blast at first but had quickly become bored and now just wanted to climb the crumbling walls of the fort's exterior. Thankfully, Eliza was happy to entertain her while Lin explored.

The tour made its way to the old jail, but the place gave Lin the creeps. The rows of empty cells looked tiny and dingy. Lin didn't want to imagine how terrifying it would have been to be imprisoned here.

The tour guide said they would have a few minutes to look around before they moved on, but Lin wasn't sure he wanted to look closer at any of the cells.

As he was glancing around, another tour group walked by, chattering, and as they passed, he noticed a man dressed in full military regalia standing in a doorway. Lin recognized the style of the uniform from the old photographs around the fort.

Probably a reenactor of some kind, Lin thought. The costume was incredibly believable. The man looked like he had stepped right out of the pictures of the troops that were here over a hundred years ago. Lin started to approach the actor, but the actor turned and quickly disappeared into the crowd.

When Lin's tour group arrived at the last stop, the courtyard in the middle of the fort, Eliza and Willow caught up with them. Willow held Eliza's hand and chattered away about all the adventuring she had done.

"Did you see the reenactor?" Lin asked.

"No, we missed that," Eliza said. "I hope there are more actors though. Willow would love it."

The tour guide finished his script.

"And as you can see, this is the location of the fort's guillotine," the tour guide said, pointing at the old rusty machine. "Deserters, thieves, and those suspected of treason were brought to judgment here in a public setting. The practice was deemed inhumane and discontinued over a century ago, but we leave it here as a reminder of the fort's checkered history."

As the tour guide thanked everyone for coming, Lin spotted the reenactor again in the corner of the courtyard.

"Look, he's over there."

Eliza looked around, even standing on her toes to see through the crowd. "I don't see him. Maybe I'm too short."

Eliza hopped up on a nearby stone wall to get a better view, and Lin put Willow on his shoulders. Still, neither could see the reenactor.

As their tour group dispersed, Eliza hopped down off the wall. As she did, Lin noticed a plaque featuring a list of names of those whose lives had been taken by the guillotine.

Scanning the rows, Lin paused. There, toward the bottom,

was his great-grandfather's name. It seemed he hadn't just died here, as their family records had shown; he had been executed.

Some of the names of the executed soldiers were accompanied by photographs, and next to his great-grandfather's name was a small, grainy picture. Lin studied it, then looked around the courtyard, searching for the reenactor. If he didn't know any better, Lin would swear they were the same person.

"Daddy! My Gabriela!"

Lin turned to find Willow's paper doll being carried by the wind back through the courtyard. His fatherly instincts kicked in, and he chased through the crowd, trying to catch the delicate doll with pink yarn hair dancing through the air.

"Got it!" he announced as he stomped his foot on the doll and reached down to pick it up. Immediately, people in the crowd began to shriek as the swoosh of an unsheathed blade echoed through the square.

He looked up and the sharp edge hovered just inches above the nape of his neck. And there was the man in uniform, holding the blade with his bare hands, blood gushing from his fingers.

Lin let out a scream and stumbled away from the guillotine. Eliza ran toward him, burying his head in her chest. Tour guides gathered around, apologizing for the accident, and the site was shut down as police were called to the scene to make a report.

"I never thanked him," Lin lamented. He looked around frantically for the actor who saved his life.

"Who do you mean?" the police officer asked.

"There! Over there!" Lin responded as he ran back toward the guillotine.

"Whoa, whoa, whoa." The officer restrained him as she gestured to her colleagues to join her. "Call a medic, please," she whispered. "Hallucinations."

"It's okay, buddy. You've had quite a scare," she said, comforting Lin. "Sit on down, and we'll take it from here."

Confused, Lin looked up to see the man in uniform across the courtyard. The ghost gave a bloody salute as the setting sun flashed against the guillotine and, in an instant, disappeared.

Molly's Dolly

We don't have enough furniture to fill this house, Jordan thought. He hadn't expected to find a new place that was so big, but the price had been unbeatable.

Jordan and his daughter, Lucy, had moved in just a few days ago, and they were already settling right in. It was a big change, moving from their apartment in the city to the sprawling suburban house.

Over the weekend, Lucy set up an elaborate tea party for all her dolls in the living room. She called Jordan in to join her.

Jordan recognized all the dolls in the room except one, a porcelain doll with dark hair in a white dress.

"Where did you get that one?" Jordan said, pointing to the doll.

"I found her in my closet," Lucy said. "Isn't she pretty?"

The doll must have belonged to the daughter of the last owners. He would have to ask his Realtor to reach out to them and see if they wanted the doll back.

After Lucy had cleaned up her tea party, she came into the kitchen and asked for a snack.

"You're in luck," Jordan said. "I just made a batch of chocolate chip cookies."

"My favorite." Lucy smiled, exposing a missing front tooth. "Can I have an extra one?"

"Just one before dinner." Jordan put a warm cookie on a plate.

"It's not for me," Lucy said. "It's for my friend."

"And who is this new friend?" Jordan asked, sure Lucy was trying to weasel her way into an extra sweet.

"Her name's Molly," Lucy replied. "She's up in my room."

Rolling his eyes, Jordan gave up. *One extra cookie won't wind her up too much.*

He put another cookie on the plate and sent Lucy up to her room to play.

When Jordan made his way upstairs with a basket of folded laundry, he paused at Lucy's closed bedroom door. Lucy was chattering away, likely to her new imaginary friend, Molly, about how she would start at a new school soon.

It sounded like there was a second voice in the room. *Who could that possibly be?* Alarmed, Jordan opened the door to find Lucy alone on the floor, coloring.

"Dinner in ten," Jordan said, assuming Lucy had to have been the one making the other voice.

"Can Molly stay for dinner?" Lucy asked, looking at the empty space next to her.

It wasn't the first time Lucy had conjured an imaginary friend, but it had been a couple of years since she had last mentioned one.

"She'll have to ask her parents," Jordan joked, leaving the door open and going to his room to drop off the laundry.

Lucy made no mention of Molly at dinner, and Jordan let the subject drop.

Jordan hadn't heard back from the Realtor yet, but that night he boxed up the doll Lucy had found so he could mail it to the old owners. Lucy had been disappointed at not being able to keep it but had relented when Jordan promised a new toy.

The next morning Jordan saw the doll propped up on Lucy's bed.

"I thought we talked about this," Jordan said, sitting on the edge of Lucy's bed. "That doll isn't yours. Why did you take it out of the box?"

"I didn't!" Lucy insisted. "It's Molly's favorite doll. She didn't want you to get rid of it."

"I'm sorry, honey. You'll have to tell Molly it's going back to its owner."

Jordan picked up the doll, brought it downstairs, and packed it back up. He went into the kitchen to start dinner, and when he returned to the living room, Jordan once again saw the doll had been taken out of the box and was now propped up on the couch. He angrily called Lucy downstairs.

Lucy looked confused by the doll's presence, but Jordan wasn't falling for it.

"You know you weren't supposed to take that doll out of the box," Jordan said. "Would you like to explain how it got there?"

"It wasn't me!" Lucy burst into angry tears. "I told Molly to leave it alone, but she wouldn't listen!"

Frustrated by the whole thing, Jordan sent Lucy up to her room, tossed the doll back inside the box, and taped it up.

The Realtor finally called back, saying the family didn't want whatever belongings they had left behind. "I would guess it reminds them too much of Molly."

"What did you just say?" Jordan asked.

"The family recently lost their daughter. I suppose it's too painful to hold on to her things."

Jordan stuttered a goodbye and hung up. He stumbled into the kitchen to find Molly's doll sitting in a chair at the kitchen table. Lucy crawled into the chair beside it.

"Can we have more cookies, Daddy?"

Married in the Morning

The sun was starting to set as Dorothy waited on the steps. The sound of horses and carriages on cobblestones echoed around her. She thought about sitting down, but she was far too excited to stay still, so instead she paced back and forth along the row of steps leading up to the church.

She had been anticipating this moment for weeks. She loved Herbert with her whole heart, and she couldn't wait to be married to him.

Her father had called her ridiculous when she told him she intended to marry Herbert. Dorothy's family were farmers, and although they weren't poor, they were still undoubtedly from a different lifestyle than Herbert's family. Herbert's family wore suits; her family wore coveralls. He would be expected to marry the daughter of an influential businessman, her mother had said, not some farm girl. His family would disown him if they found out he was courting a girl like her.

But Herbert had insisted he didn't care whether she had money or not. He said he didn't care that his own parents had laughed when he told them his plans to marry Dorothy. He told her he loved her, and that was all that mattered.

After weeks of trying fruitlessly to get their families to come around to the idea, Dorothy and Herbert had decided to elope.

Who cares if our parents disagree? she thought. *Nothing will stop us from being together.*

Tonight was the night her whole life would start, and Dorothy couldn't wait. She didn't have a white dress; instead, she had worn her favorite: a simple dress in a soft pink with puffed velvet sleeves.

Herbert was two hours late, but Dorothy didn't let that discourage her. She wouldn't be surprised if his family was delaying him. She knew he would come, so she didn't worry.

She wished she had decided to wait inside the church because the December air had a brutal chill to it. *I could go in,* she thought, *but if Herbert doesn't see me on the steps, he'll think I've left.*

They had agreed to meet on the steps, so the steps were where she would wait.

The sun went down, and a light snow started as night fell.

Her dress turned damp, sending a shiver through her body, but she refused to give up her patient vigil.

Her nose ran from the cold, and she took out the handkerchief she always kept with her. It was Herbert's, monogrammed with an *H*. He had given it to her, and she kept it as a reminder of him when he wasn't with her.

When exhaustion set in, she finally sat down on the damp, snowy steps, wrapping her arms around herself. She felt unbelievably tired, and fear started to creep in that maybe Herbert wasn't coming after all.

Impossible, she told herself. *Herbert loves me. There must be a perfectly reasonable explanation for why he isn't here.* Dorothy refused to believe that he wouldn't arrive any minute.

I just have to keep waiting, she told herself. *So what if we're delayed another day? We'll be married in the morning.*

The snow continued, falling heavy and wet around her, and she felt tired deep in her bones.

As her eyes started to droop closed, she whispered into the night, "I'm waiting, Herbert."

The next morning the priest found her body on the steps, frozen to death from exposure to the elements overnight.

Sofia took the steps up to the church two at a time. She was running thirty minutes late and was barely looking where she was going.

She and her fiancé were supposed to be wed at 5:00 p.m., but traffic was a mess, and the final touches on her hair took a bit longer than expected. *It's worth it,* she thought. *He'll see.*

Sofia had a reputation for running behind schedule, which drove her fiancé mad. They say opposites attract, and Sofia and Tomas couldn't have been more opposite. He was the yin to her yang, and that's what made them work so well. She even had a joke about it in her vows, which she rehearsed under her breath as she ran up the church stairs. In true Sofia fashion, she had just written them last night and was still working to memorize them.

Head down, rushing to the front door, Sofia tripped and just caught herself before she fell onto the cement steps.

"I'm so sorry," Sofia apologized as she looked up to find a lovely, frail woman crouched on the steps. It was her who Sofia had stumbled over. "I wasn't looking where I was going. Are you okay?"

"I'm wonderful." The woman gave her a soft smile.

Sofia stepped to the side and plowed ahead, taking the stairs one at a time now. Even in her haste, she couldn't help but notice the woman was wearing a long pink dress with voluminous velvet sleeves. It would be hot in that outfit, given that the summer day was well over ninety degrees.

She must be sweating to death, Sofia thought.

The heavy wooden door to the church creaked when Sofia opened it. She turned to the woman on the steps and gestured forward.

"Are you coming inside?" Sofia asked. It was only polite for her to hold the door open for her.

The woman had begun pacing back and forth on the steps. She waved Sofia on, barely looking in her direction.

"No," she said. "I'm waiting for someone."

Sofia entered the church and loudly announced her arrival, joking about her evergreen tardiness. "Look, Tomas knew what he was getting into," she joked to the small group of lingering attendees congregating in the foyer. "So if he's mad, that's on him!"

"Have you seen him?" the priest inquired.

"Tomas? Of course not! It's bad luck," Sofia explained as a tinge of fear rushed through her bones. "Why? Is he not here?"

"Not yet. We were hoping you would know where he was. Perhaps he's outside."

"No, there's just some lady in a dress with puffy velvet sleeves out on the steps. Trust me. I tripped over her."

The priest's face dropped, and he rushed out the door. Confused at his reaction, Sofia followed him, but the woman with the puffy sleeves was nowhere to be seen. On the steps Sofia noticed a white handkerchief embroidered with the letter *H* lying where the woman had been. The priest picked it up, gently folding it into a square.

"I'm so sorry, Sofia," he whispered in a low, somber tone, pushing the handkerchief into her hands. "You can wait all you want, but I'm afraid Tomas will not be marrying you today."

Jailbreak

"Don't be such babies," Kyle said as he lifted the flashlight beam in front of him. "I've been here dozens of times."

"I heard it was haunted," Zach answered, nervous.

"I don't believe in ghosts," Ian declared. "But I do believe in cops. Aren't we trespassing?"

Kyle shrugged. "Maybe, technically. But nobody is keeping an eye on this place. And like I said, I've been here before."

Kyle had bragged to Ian and Zach about how he had spent the night at the old county jail, but Ian had just laughed and said Kyle probably only lasted five minutes.

It was a bit of a local tradition for teenagers to try to spend the night at "County," but Ian had never been tempted to try.

Zach had come once before nightfall but had left without even giving the challenge a chance.

Only Kyle claimed to have completed the rite of passage, and he had urged the other two to toughen up and try it.

Tonight, the sky was completely clear, but it was a new moon, and the darkness engulfed everything in shadow.

Twigs and leaves crunched under their feet as they trudged forward. The old jail was surrounded by a chain-link fence topped with barbed wire, but there were plenty of holes if you knew where to look.

Kyle led the way, moving aside some branches and ducking through an opening in the fence. Ian followed, and after a moment of hesitation, Zach joined them.

Ian had seen the crumbling jail building hundreds of times through a car window, but up close it looked much more imposing. The abandoned building was covered with cracked windows and graffiti, and knee-high brush had grown over all the pathways.

The wind picked up, and Ian could hear thumps and banging from inside the building. He paused, listening.

"Just a bunch of old debris flying around, I bet," Kyle said.

Undeterred, he slammed a shoulder into the huge front door, shoving it open with an ominous creak. "Should we split up?" Kyle joked as they walked inside.

The only light came from the flashlights they each carried, and they had to walk slowly so they didn't trip over cracks in the floor or debris in their way.

Now that they were inside, Ian could hear the noises much more clearly. The banging and rattling sounded like cell doors opening and closing. They made their way into the first section of cells. Ian couldn't feel any wind here, but the doors to most of the cells had been left open.

Some of the cells had graffiti or leftover garbage from other teenagers who had been there. Zach stood in the hallway for a while, too unsettled by the scene to move forward. Ian stepped into one of the cells to get a closer look. Kyle joined him.

"I wish we had brought some spray paint," Kyle commented. "Could've graffitied our names."

"I don't think I want to leave my name here." Zach shook his head. "In fact, maybe we should just leave."

"Let's give it a little longer," Ian said, feeling a little braver now that they were inside and it just looked like any other abandoned building. "We don't have to stay the whole night, but you have to admit it's kind of cool."

Zach said nothing.

"What's the matter?" Kyle laughed. "Afraid the ghosts will get you?"

The sound of a door slamming clanged through the hallway, but Ian couldn't see where it came from.

"Don't be mean, Kyle," Ian said, a little unnerved by the sound.

"Oh, come on! Don't tell me you're falling for this ghost thing," Kyle scoffed.

The banging resumed, and Ian could see a door a few cells away slam shut. Then he heard another slam. And another. One by one, the doors of the cells leading down to where they were standing slammed closed.

The doors closed so quickly that before Ian and Kyle could

react, the door to the cell they were standing in slammed, closing them in. Ian ran forward, shaking the bars, but it wouldn't budge.

"Very funny, Zach," Kyle said.

"I didn't do that!" Zach shouted. "Maybe the ghosts weren't a fan of you insulting them. Ever think of that?"

"Maybe instead of insulting each other, we could work on getting out of here?" Ian said, trying ineffectively to get the door to open.

Zach pushed, Ian and Kyle pulled, but no matter what they did, they remained trapped. The wind started to pick up, howling through the hallway.

All three flashlights went out at the same time, plunging them into darkness. A shriek pierced the air.

"Okay, okay!" Kyle cried. "I'm sorry. I shouldn't have insulted the ghosts."

The wind died down, and the flashlights flickered back to life. And there, on the wall of the graffiti, were all three of their names, dripping in fresh red paint.

With another bang, all the cell doors in the hallway opened simultaneously.

Panicking, Zach ran from the cell block, followed by the others.

"Don't want to stay the night?" Ian prodded, his breath coming sharp and quick from fear.

"You know . . . I'm good," Kyle sputtered as he sprinted back toward the entrance.

IAN

The Night Nurse

Mary always tried her best to be extra kind to the new patients. It was hard enough being admitted, and Mary knew they would be missing their families and feeling confused about their new surroundings. In a way, she felt like a mother figure to them.

The Westview Hospital for the Mentally Ill was Mary's home in almost every sense of the word. She had been working here since the day she became a nurse in 1908. It had been twenty years now, and she had never married or had any children. Mary had devoted her entire life to her career. She worked the overnight shift, and she was perfectly happy with her situation.

One of the other nurses had mentioned that they had a

new patient, Henry. It would be his first night there, and Mary wanted to make sure he was comfortable. Or as comfortable as could be, given the circumstances.

Before entering Henry's room, Mary stopped to read through the chart posted on his door. He was suffering from visual and auditory hallucinations, according to the notes, and there was a warning that he could turn violent if frightened. *That's a shame*, Mary thought, *but it was not too unusual for new patients to be angry about coming here.* Usually, it was their parents or loved ones who brought them in.

She gave a quick, light knock before walking into the room.

"Who's there?" Henry sat up in the bed, and his head turned toward the door. When he spotted Mary, his eyes bulged. "Who are you?"

"It's all right, Henry." Mary used her softest, most soothing tone. "My name is Mary. I'm one of the nurses here."

"No more nurses. No more doctors." Henry moaned. He had been put in a straitjacket upon admittance. Mary always thought the restraint was a bit cruel, but it was often necessary the first night. She had seen more than one patient try to hurt themselves or one of the staff.

"You can just think of me as a friend," Mary said, moving a bit closer to the bed. "Someone to talk to."

"A friend?" Henry's eyes looked glazed and tired, and a bead of sweat slipped down his forehead.

When Mary left his room later that night, she felt like she had established a good rapport with Henry. At times, he would get nervous, looking away and saying he saw a person or an animal or a monster in the corner. When he did, Mary talked

to him calmly, reminding him where he was and who she was until he settled down.

She went back to his room every night for the next few nights, and by the end of the week she thought she was making real progress with him. He was calmer, more open, and happier than he had been when he arrived.

Mary was in Henry's room one night when they were interrupted by a doctor barging through the door. She hadn't realized what time it was; it must have been nearly breakfast time. Mary recognized Dr. Lester.

"All right, Henry, medication time." Dr. Lester laid out a small tray of pills and a cup of water next to the bed. "Then a nurse will be in to take you to breakfast."

"Couldn't Nurse Mary take me?" Henry gestured at Mary. "She's already here."

Mary was a little annoyed that she'd been completely unacknowledged by the doctor, but that happened sometimes.

Dr. Lester jolted, then looked over to the corner where Mary was standing. He blinked a few times, shaking his head. When he spoke again, his voice was angry.

"I'm not sure who told you about Mary, but they shouldn't be filling your head with nonsense. Clearly, your hallucinations are getting worse. I'll have to adjust your medication."

Dr. Lester stormed out, and Mary walked quickly behind him, calling at him to wait a minute.

"Did one of you mention Mary to the patient in room 351?" Dr. Lester berated the nurses at the station.

"Excuse me!" Mary shouted, but Dr. Lester went on as if she weren't even there.

"Why would we have done that?" Gloria, who had worked alongside Mary for the better half of a decade, spoke up. "It's been years since she died. Her name wouldn't come up in casual conversation with patients."

What on earth is going on here? Mary wondered. *Has someone put the doctor up to this as a prank of some kind? Or perhaps he's confusing me with someone else.*

"Since I what?" Mary stepped forward.

Once again, nobody paid her any mind.

"Well, someone must have mentioned her," Dr. Lester continued. "Because the patient in 351 is having hallucinations and said Mary was in his room. He wouldn't be saying that if someone hadn't told him about her. I don't want him running around telling the other patients he sees a dead woman."

Dr. Lester huffed his way down the hall, muttering under his breath. One of the younger nurses, a woman Mary didn't recognize, was visibly distraught.

"Who's Mary?" she asked Gloria.

"I am!" Mary insisted. "And I would appreciate it if you stopped this practical joke. For goodness' sake, Gloria, this has gone too far."

Mary slammed her hand down on the desk in front of her, but to her shock, her palm went right through the surface. It was as if her hand wasn't even there. She looked down at her hands in confusion.

"She used to be a nurse here," Gloria said sadly. "She loved this job. She was working when she died. Such a shame."

Shaking her head in horror, Mary backed away slowly, then turned and ran down the hallway to Henry's room.

"Do you see me?" she pleaded as she burst into the room.

"I do. Is that bad?" he asked in a hushed tone.

"I think so."

The Last Word

Every time John and Felix were put on the same shift, they got into a fight, bickering like brothers. While neither of them took their spats seriously, the rest of the crew loathed when they worked together.

One thing their friendship guaranteed: volume. Lots and lots of volume. And after a few hours on the job, they became obnoxious to be around. Both of them were always determined to get the last word in, and their arguments could go on for hours and hours.

Today, as they worked from scaffolding at the top of the lighthouse, they argued over which team had played the best in last night's game. It didn't matter that John's team had lost to Felix's favorite. As far as John was concerned, they had been robbed.

"You're out of your mind if you think Jones didn't deserve that flag!" Felix shouted.

"That ref had it in for them!" John defended.

"Whatya talking about? He grabbed the quarterback's face mask."

"Never touched him!"

"You gotta get your eyes checked! I can't believe they let you work here when you can't even see straight."

The fight continued, with the men's voices echoing down the hollow tower of the lighthouse. They had been working on this repair project for weeks. The old lighthouse in the harbor had endured a lot of weather damage over the years. It had been closed for a decade, but the town was eager to get it up and running again.

This week's project was the exterior at the top of the lighthouse, which was desperately in need of masonry repairs. Felix and John were nearly a hundred feet up on their shared scaffold, working on a section together.

Although he'd never admit it, John was afraid of heights, and this particular project was a lot taller than he was used to. He frequently double-checked the carabiner on his belt, which clipped him to a safety line.

Quite a few of the workers were packing up for the night, but with rain coming soon, John and Felix agreed (for once) that it was best to push through and put in a little overtime.

"Let's get this job done. Then I won't have to see your stupid face again tomorrow." John jabbed Felix in the back.

John couldn't say exactly how it had happened. As Felix turned to take a step toward him, he tripped over himself and threw out his hands. With a thud, Felix landed face down.

John steadied himself, then reached down to offer Felix a hand. But Felix didn't move. A small puddle of blood started pooling on the platform.

He nudged Felix, but there was still no response. Then he saw it: a hammer on the ground where Felix had fallen, covered in blood. He must have landed right on top of it, hitting his head.

Panic started to snake through John. There was a lot of blood now, and Felix didn't look like he was breathing. John reached down to take his pulse, but there was no heartbeat.

Felix was dead.

What am I supposed to do? How am I going to explain this? John wondered in a panic.

Nobody would ever believe Felix had fallen and landed on a hammer. It sounded absurd. And the fights they got into were well-known among their coworkers. Everyone would think John had hit him. They would say he had murdered Felix. Terror crawled up John's throat and clouded his vision. The fear consumed John so completely that he wasn't thinking straight. All he knew was that he had to make sure everyone knew it was an accident.

He reached down and unclipped the tether that attached Felix to the safety line. Then John, with a lump in his throat, pushed Felix's body right over the scaffolding. The body finally reached the ground with a sickening, echoing thud, and then John frantically called for help.

The remaining crew came rushing over. Some were shouting, one was calling for an ambulance, and two others helped John down from the scaffolding.

"Felix fell," John eventually told the police, "and his safety clip wasn't attached properly. There was nothing I could have done to stop him from falling."

That's what John kept telling himself the rest of the night and well into the early morning hours. *I couldn't have done anything.*

John sat by himself at the kitchen counter as the clock ticked toward 3:00 a.m., unable to fall asleep. He had poured himself a strong drink, then a second, but he couldn't stop replaying the moment in his mind when he had pushed Felix over the edge of the scaffolding. He finally started to feel his eyes droop, and he hoped sleep would consume him soon.

A chill ran down John's spine as he heard a whispered voice behind him.

"I wasn't dead, John."

John spun around, but there was nobody else in the kitchen.

John recognized the voice. *Impossible*, he thought. *Felix was definitely dead. I checked his pulse.*

Doubt started nagging John as he poured yet another drink, chugging it down and trying to drown out the words.

He had been dead, right? John wouldn't have shoved the body off the scaffolding if Felix wasn't dead. His hands started shaking and tears filled his eyes. What had he done?

The next morning John returned to the construction site, determined to finish the work he and Felix had started.

Others offered to help, but John insisted on working alone. He couldn't have any more accidents. And he wasn't ready to talk about the loss of his friend.

It was an agonizing day, but John finally finished and packed up all his materials. His body was aching, and he was ready to sink into his well-worn couch and distract himself with whatever he found on TV.

As he climbed down the edge of the scaffold, the voice once again rang in his ears.

"I wasn't dead, John."

John looked up just in time to see a hammer spiraling toward him, knocking him to the ground.

Felix got the last word, after all.

Rockabye

Thunder crashed as Nina's car rumbled over the little wooden bridge. Rain was pelting the windshield faster than the wipers could keep up, and she could barely see more than a foot ahead of her. It took all her focus to make sure the car didn't skid off the bridge into the choppy waters below.

I should have left earlier, Nina lectured herself, *and then I wouldn't have been caught in this storm.* She was the only one foolish enough to be out on the road at this hour. She was supposed to be more responsible now that she was a mother. Caleb was only three months old, and she already felt like she was messing up constantly.

A very disgruntled Caleb was screaming his head off in

the back seat. The thunder and the rumble of the bridge had woken him from his nap.

She tried her typical lullabies, but he didn't stop crying. Nina could see in the rearview mirror that he had dropped his favorite stuffed toy, a little blue dog, on the floor.

"Shh, I know," Nina soothed, reaching back with one hand to pat his leg in comfort.

Caleb kept right on wailing.

Focusing back on the road, Nina saw a shape in the beam of her headlights.

A woman was standing in the middle of the road.

Nina slammed on the brakes. The car jolted to a stop, making Caleb cry even harder.

She checked to make sure Caleb was okay. *Oh, thank goodness.* When Nina looked back to the road, the woman was gone.

"What the . . . ?" Nina squinted through the pouring rain, trying to see where the woman had gone. *Maybe she was just crossing the street,* Nina thought. She couldn't see her anywhere ahead.

Or maybe the lack of sleep was getting to her. Caleb still woke several times during the night, and Nina was constantly exhausted. Perhaps she had just imagined the woman.

Confused, she decided it was best to take a break from driving for a minute or two. She eased the car to the side of the road, putting it in Park. Caleb was inconsolable now, despite her best attempts at shushing and patting. Nina debated getting into the back seat with him.

The radio turned staticky, then started rapidly switching

from one station to another. The sound was shrill and grating. Nina jabbed the power button, but the radio wouldn't turn off.

Frustrated, she unbuckled her seat belt so she could get closer to Caleb, whose crying had reached ear-shattering volumes. The radio continued crackling and changing, and nothing Nina tried could get it to shut off.

Thunder cracked, and the woman appeared again, closer now, with rain dripping down her dark hair. Nina didn't think she was wearing a raincoat or using an umbrella. She must have been cold.

Caleb kept screaming. She turned on the overhead light, twisting behind her and sticking her arm down to the floor of the back seat, desperately hoping the dropped toy would be within arm's reach.

The car jolted, and Nina whipped her head around to see a streak across the window closest to Caleb as if a hand had smacked it.

Absolutely nobody is getting near my baby, Nina thought. She moved quickly, flinging open her door and jumping out, frantically looking around the car. She ran to stand protectively in front of Caleb's door. There was nobody in sight, though the rain made it harder to tell for sure. The water quickly seeped into Nina's sneakers as she opened the back door and leaned in, adjusting Caleb's blanket and trying to calm him without letting too much rain in.

She found his stuffed dog and handed it to him. His cries quieted slightly, but he continued sniffling.

Nina stood, feeling like someone was nearby. Warily, she turned her head.

Standing not five feet away from her was the woman Nina had seen on the road. She was wearing nothing but a white nightgown, her feet bare, her hair dripping. Nina watched as the woman looked right past her, zoning in on Caleb.

The woman took a step forward. There was something off about her beyond her harried appearance. The edges of her body shimmered and warped slightly like she was only partially in this world.

Terrified, Nina shifted, blocking the woman's access to Caleb.

The woman let out a soul-shattering scream, then stepped forward again, looking past Nina.

Nina recognized the grief and pain in her scream. A mother's scream.

An idea struck Nina.

She held up her hands. "He's not your baby."

The woman looked back at Nina, confusion on her face, and then stopped.

Nina nodded toward Caleb. "He's not your baby," she repeated. "I'm so sorry."

The woman took one more step, but her demeanor had changed enough that Nina thought it was safe to let her get closer. Sadness shadowed the woman's eyes as she stared at Caleb.

Heartbreak was written across her sallow, ghostly face. The woman cried out again, a melancholy wail, then dissolved into the descending rain. The radio hushed, leaving behind an eerie silence in its wake.

Nina didn't know when she had started crying, but she

couldn't seem to stop. Hands shaking, she kissed Caleb and wiped his tears. Then she got back in the driver's seat and drove away as fast as she dared. She resumed her soothing nursery rhymes and bedtime songs, but she would never drown out the memory of the ghostly mother's shriek, desperately searching for her little one.

"Quiet, Please"

Maya had stayed at the library way later than she meant to. She had a final tomorrow, and she needed to go home and get a good night's sleep. It was now nearing midnight, and she was the last person on this floor of the university library.

Maya had always hated studying here. It gave her the creeps at night, and she had heard the librarians were incredibly strict, so she preferred to study somewhere else. Maya wasn't the only one who felt like this place was a little odd. One of her friends insisted it was haunted and would never come in at all. Maya didn't take the feeling too seriously, so she had agreed when her study group had wanted to meet here. It had just made sense to stay where she was when they were done, so Maya had settled in for a night of cramming.

Her eyes started to droop as she stared at the page in front of her, and she knew if she didn't leave soon, she would fall asleep on top of the table. She propped her head on her fist and closed her eyes, promising herself she would just rest them for a minute and then she'd leave.

One minute turned into five, and Maya dozed off until a thud startled her. She bolted upright, blinking the sleep away, and saw that the thud had come from a book that had fallen off the table from the top of a stack that was precariously close to the edge.

Good thing that noise woke me up, Maya thought, because she had knocked over her water bottle, which was now leaving a growing puddle on the table that was inching closer to the corner of her book.

With a shouted curse, Maya moved the book out of the way, righted the bottle, and ran to get a stack of paper towels from the bathroom to clean up the spill. Someone whispered an annoyed "Shh!" at the sound of her shout. *Weird*, Maya thought. She hadn't realized anyone else was still in this area of the library.

Maya quickly wiped up the mess and decided it was time for her to go home. She shoved the book back on the shelf quickly, not paying attention to exactly where it went, and then accidentally kicked up a cloud of dust.

A sneezing fit overtook Maya as the dust reached her nose, and she heard another "Shh!" from somewhere behind her. *Rude*. She couldn't exactly help it if she needed to sneeze.

As she packed up her belongings and put up the rest of the books she'd been using, a message pinged on her phone loudly. She hadn't realized the volume was up, but the alert sounded shrill in the quiet of the library.

A man appeared beside Maya, a bearded, bald sort with a stern face. He was wearing a well-fitted tweed vest, paired with a navy-blue suit with brown patches on the elbows and a tie cinched tightly around his neck. Maya had no idea where the man had come from.

He extended his finger inches away from her nose. Petrified, Maya stumbled backward, tripping over her own feet and bumping her back up against one of the bookshelves behind her. She was still clutching one of the books she had been returning between her hands.

"I warned you twice now, so consider this your third offense." The man's voice was raspy. "Quiet, please, in my library."

The man's face turned grotesque, and it looked like his skin was melting right off him. His pointed finger became warped and bent, and the bone poked out through the rapidly rotting skin. Maya screamed in horror, twisting her head and raising the book in front of her in defense.

The scream only served to make the man angrier, and he reached his bony hand toward Maya's throat. Whether he meant to choke her or threaten her, Maya didn't know, because she lifted the book and smashed it into the ghastly ghost's face. The man turned to dust before her eyes, swirling into a black cloud that dissipated into the air.

No classwork or test score was *this* important. Maya

dropped the book on the ground, bolted out of the library, and decided once and for all that she was never coming back here to study again.

All That Glitters

"And you're sure you didn't just misplace them?" Jeremiah asked the guest. A long line was forming behind her.

"See, this is why I needed to talk to a manager," Mrs. Farley insisted. "He's calling me a liar."

"Ma'am, I assure you that I don't think you're lying," Sonia, the front desk manager, said with a withering stare at Jeremiah. He took a step back, rolling his eyes. Usually, he was patient with guests, so Sonia knew something must have set him off. "Can you tell me what's wrong?"

"I already told the front desk boy. I want to make a report about what happened in my room last night—room 216," Mrs. Farley huffed. "My earrings are missing. I took them off last night, and when I woke up this morning, they were gone."

"I understand how frustrating this must be," Sonia said, trying to placate the elderly woman.

"Someone stole them," Mrs. Farley insisted.

"But you were there the whole time?" Jeremiah prompted. "You never left your room?"

"I did not, young man, and I would remember. I am not old," Mrs. Farley clapped back. "I think housekeeping stole them. I can show you where they were."

Sonia begrudgingly followed Mrs. Farley to the second floor to one of the most beautiful rooms the hotel had to offer, which had been formerly inhabited by one of the hotel owner's children. The room featured twelve-foot ceilings and ornately arched doorways. It was decorated with a king-size, four-poster bed with gilded sconces on either side. The tasseled curtains were closed tight, and the room was dark. And there, sure enough, was a pair of ruby earrings on the bedside table.

"I'm telling you that they weren't there an hour ago. Those hooligans must have gotten nervous and put them back," a red-faced Mrs. Farley conceded. With a profuse amount of apologizing from Sonia and a discount on her stay, Mrs. Farley was eventually satisfied and checked out of the hotel.

"Some people will say anything to save some cash," Jeremiah said after Mrs. Farley left. "What a bogus story."

Sonia loved working at the hotel, despite the frequency of guest complaints. More often than not, the guests were happy and excited to stay in the historic hotel. It had been run by the same family for generations.

Later that day, Sonia got a complaint from the housekeeping staff. When they went in to clean, they said that a child was sitting in a room that was supposed to be empty. The child had scared the daylights out of the workers, who wanted to know why the front desk had marked that room as empty when there was a guest in it.

Sonia apologized and promised to look into it, then pulled up the records for the room. Number 216.

"Are you sure that's the number?"

"Of course," the housekeeper replied.

"It is empty. I checked the woman out myself this morning."

"I assure you that there is a child sitting up there who will not budge."

Sonia visited the room. No one was there. She took a look around, turning on all the lights and drawing open the curtains. She checked in drawers, under the bed, and in the closet. She even inspected the bathroom, peering behind the shower curtain, leaving no space unturned. The woman who'd been there the night before hadn't left anything behind, and there was no sign that anyone had been in there without permission.

When she stepped out of the bathroom, Sonia let out a shrill, high-pitched scream. A young girl was sitting on the bed wearing Sonia's earrings. Sonia clutched her earlobes. Although she hadn't taken them off, the pair of gold hoops had disappeared from her lobes,

"Don't move," Sonia said to the child, moving to block the door. "I'm calling security."

She took out her phone, pulling up the contact for the security desk. Sonia's mind raced, looking for any explanation for what she was seeing. *Thief? Hallucination? Magician?*

Ghost?

"This is security," a man answered.

Before Sonia could find the words, the girl on the bed began screeching with laughter. Then suddenly the specter disappeared, and Sonia's earrings dropped on the floor with a clatter.

"Hello?" the man replied.

Sonia hung up the phone, snatched the earrings from the floor, and hastily shoved them into her pocket as she bolted back to the front desk.

"Are you okay?" Jeremiah asked when he saw Sonia's ashen face. "You look like you might be sick."

Sonia felt a bit nauseated but decided to keep the story to herself. No one would believe her, and she still wasn't sure what she had seen. At the end of the day, she decided to retire to the hotel dining room for a late-night snack. As she ate, she studied the portraits on the wall. She'd never taken the time to appreciate her surroundings, but a large painting over the mantel caught her eye. The hotel's first owner and his family. He had seven daughters, and all of them were painted around him and his wife.

Sonia scanned the portrait, noticing the humble dresses and stark faces of the bunch—clearly, a family with many mouths to feed, unable to afford much excess. With one exception. The youngest daughter sat cross-legged in the corner of the photo and was covered in jewelry, with rings on nearly every finger, thick bracelets laced with emeralds and rubies on her wrists, and a gaudy diamond necklace around her neck.

Sonia reached into her pocket, placed her earrings on the mantel, and excused herself for the evening.

The next morning when she returned to the hotel, the earrings had disappeared. But Sonia couldn't help but smile when she saw the portrait. The little girl's face had an extra glow this morning as she was wearing her new pair of gold hoops.

Beware the Reaper

George had been excited when he got the call for this job. This particular cemetery was at least 150 years old and filled with stone mausoleums big enough to fit a studio apartment inside. *There must be dozens of descendants in each one*, George thought. It was bigger than most cemeteries within a hundred miles, and the job would be his biggest to date, one he could make a significant profit on.

George and his sister, Sharon, co-owned the small landscaping company, but the real brains of the operation was their cousin, Laura, their honorary partner. Laura had lived with them in their teenage years, and she was like a sister to them.

Now adults, they all lived within a five-mile radius, and they were the only remaining family in the Hannagan clan.

Laura already had a full-time job, but when she saw George and Sharon drowning in all the paperwork, she offered to help them out. She pulled in as many jobs and logged as many hours as either of them. No other employee was as involved or as invested in their success.

They parked the company van just inside the gate, and the three of them unloaded lawn mowers and tools. It would take hours to get through this gig, but George just smiled to himself as he popped on his headphones and got to work.

"Did you see the creepy reaper statue?" Laura asked when they met back up for lunch. "I don't know why anyone would want something that morbid on their grave."

George shrugged. He hadn't seen the statue, but he wasn't surprised there were a few odd grave markers.

"Not the weirdest we've seen," Sharon said. "Remember the dolphin statue?"

"Or the one where they carved emojis for the epitaph?" George recalled.

They continued naming the strangest headstones they had seen, making it a competition over who had seen the best one.

"Even if it wasn't the winner," Laura said before they went back to work, suddenly much more serious, "there was something off about that reaper statue. When I looked in its eyes, time stopped and I saw myself having a heart attack."

"Have you had enough water today? Maybe you need some protein?" Sharon suggested.

Laura declined, and the three of them went back to work.

But by the end of that week, Laura looked like she had barely slept.

"I think I might be going crazy," she confessed to George when he asked if she was all right. "Do you remember what I told you I saw when I looked at that statue?"

When George nodded, she continued. "I can't stop thinking about having a heart attack. I keep seeing that vision over and over."

"Why don't you bow out for the rest of this job? Sharon and I can handle it."

Laura happily agreed.

The next morning George set out early before dawn to see the statue for himself. He found it towering over a grave beneath a gnarled old tree. The statue was life-size, reaching a few inches over George's head. The reaper had been carved with a swirling cloak and hood over his head, and he was carrying a large, imposing scythe.

Part of the reaper's head was visible beneath the hood, and the sculptor had carved wide, empty eyes in its face.

George looked into those blank eyes, and then he felt it. Time stopped, and the world disappeared around him. He saw himself sitting behind his truck's steering wheel as an eighteen-wheeler drove straight into him.

George jumped back, letting out a yelp and dropping the pruning shears he had been using to trim the tree's overhanging leaves.

Now George knew why Laura had been so freaked out. He wanted to tell Sharon and Laura but was afraid they might think he, too, was losing his mind.

Later that night, when he went to sleep, the vision hit him again. He sat straight up in bed, terrified. He needed to talk to someone. Just as he started to pick up the phone to call Laura, it began to ring. George answered it.

Laura's husband was on the other line. Laura had been taken to the hospital. She'd had a heart attack. She hadn't survived.

Unable to find the right words, George thanked Laura's husband and hung up the phone. It wasn't long before Sharon was at his door, each trying to comfort the other.

The funeral came and went, but the sorrow over Laura lingered. And George's fear did too.

He told Sharon about how he had gone to see the reaper, the same one that haunted Laura, and the vision he had about the accident. She dismissed it, but George could not be swayed.

He spent the next year of his life avoiding driving, which was no small feat for his rural area of town. He'd ask Sharon to pick him up and for neighbors to grab his groceries. He'd often walk on foot if he had to, sometimes upwards of ten miles. The neighbors excused his odd behavior as grief, but he knew Laura's death wasn't a coincidence; it was fate. And he was determined to avoid his. Walk if he must, but he would not get behind the wheel of a vehicle.

That is, until Sharon called him, panicked, needing a ride to the hospital. She was in labor, her husband was out of town, and he was the only family she had nearby.

"Please. I'm desperate."

"Okay." George sighed. "I'm coming."

Sharon sat, hunched over her swollen belly, trying to breathe through the pain. What was taking him so long? Sharon called George again and again, but it went straight to voicemail.

"I can't believe you!" she screamed angrily at her phone after a half hour of waiting.

A few moments later Sharon heard a siren whirring past her window. Then another. And another. She looked outside to see a chorus of police cars gathered around the bend, followed shortly by an ambulance.

Wailing in pain and still furious at George for abandoning her, she stumbled out the door, begging an officer to help her. And then she saw it—George's landscaping truck crumpled under the weight of an eighteen-wheeler. Her tears turned to tears of grief, and the police officer caught her in his arms.

Four hours later, Sharon was still sobbing as she welcomed twins: George and Laura.

Here Comes the Bride

Lily had been waiting for this her whole life. She stared into the golden, floor-length mirror, admiring herself in the white dress. Bridal shopping was even more fun than Lily had imagined. She loved trying on the different shapes and styles. Currently, she was wearing a ball gown with enough tulle that the skirt could stand up on its own.

"You look great. Like a cupcake, but great." Hana, Lily's best friend, sat sipping a glass of champagne. "But I feel like you can't pick the dress until you have the ring."

"I'll have it soon." Lily rolled her eyes. "And engaged is engaged."

She would have to nudge Leo about a ring soon. Lily had been so excited, so overwhelmed when he had said he wanted to marry her, that she had said yes immediately. So what if it wasn't some big planned proposal with a ring? It was still romantic to Lily, and now she would get to pick out a ring herself, so in some ways it was a good thing.

"I'm glad Leo came around," Hana said, downing the rest of her glass. "When you said last week that his ex-fiancée had reached out, I was worried it would strain your relationship, but it seems like it just made you stronger."

Lily had been furious when she had caught Leo on the phone with his ex, Paige. Lily had thrown his phone across the room, shattering the screen in her rage.

Losing was something Lily had never experienced, and she wasn't about to start with Leo. She had known then that there was no way she would let him go back to Paige. She would do everything in her power to make sure he was hers.

Leo had insisted it meant nothing. He said he loved Lily and wanted to be with her.

She had angrily accused him of placating her, but he had said he wanted to marry her, and she had calmed instantly, agreeing on the spot.

"I think you need more sparkle," Hana said, interrupting Lily's thoughts. Hana grabbed one of the other hangers in the dressing room. "Try this one."

As Hana helped her into the next dress, Lily drifted back to thinking about Paige.

After she calmed down about Leo talking to Paige on the phone, Lily had called her, but Paige had shut her down.

"My conversations with Leo are none of your business," Paige had fumed before hanging up on Lily.

There had been no other choice, really, but for Lily to go over to Paige's apartment. Lily had managed to track down the address online. Paige had been surprised to see her, but Lily had insisted on coming inside.

It wasn't Lily's fault that the conversation had gotten so heated. Paige was delusional, and Lily needed to shake some sense into her.

"You're old news!" Lily had shouted. "He doesn't want to be with you."

Paige had laughed. "You don't have a clue what you're talking about. We never even broke up. You're just a mistake."

Lily had been surprised by the statement, but she quickly decided Paige was a liar. Leo had said he broke up with Paige and had insisted he loved Lily. She knew Leo would never lie to her. It was Paige who couldn't be trusted.

"Oooh, this one needs a veil," Hana cheered, pulling Lily back to the present.

When she turned around, she thought she looked radiant. The dress was a perfect fit, and the veil completed the picture.

"You look like a bride," Hana said. "I'm getting teary."

Hana went to get a tissue while Lily studied herself in the mirror.

I showed her, Lily thought. *I'm the one he's marrying. I won.*

She watched in the mirror as a red stain on her stomach spread over her dress. It looked like blood spilling out in her reflection, but when she looked down, there wasn't a mark on the dress. It was pure white.

When she looked up, Lily saw a woman standing behind her in the mirror.

"Paige?"

Lily turned, but nobody was there. She turned back to the mirror, the image of Paige standing behind her and the blood spilling down her dress still there.

As Hana came back in the room, a tissue in one hand and her phone in the other, the image of Paige leaned in and whispered to Lily, "Murderer," before she disappeared.

"You won't believe this," Hana said, waving her phone toward Lily. "Leo is all over the news. Look."

She handed Lily the phone with a news article pulled up.

"His ex was found murdered in her apartment," Hana said. "They said she was stabbed, but there's no murder weapon."

Lily read the headline, "Murderer at Large."

The article even quoted Leo: "I'm 100 percent committed to helping the police find whoever killed Paige. My fiancée deserves justice," he had said.

Lily looked back up from the phone to her reflection, still covered in blood only she could see.

"Do you want to answer this?" Hana asked as she picked up Lily's ringing phone from the dressing room chair. "It's Leo."

Under the Surface

The camp looked exactly as Jess remembered. She had spent every summer from ages nine to sixteen here, but she had been nervous when she got the invite for a ten-year reunion. Her last summer here had ended in tragedy when there was an accident at the lake. The camp had closed down early, and she hadn't come back since.

As she checked in for the weekend, she wondered who would be sharing her cabin. She had already talked to Ashley, who should be arriving soon, and promised to save the bed next to hers.

After she unpacked, she made her way to the mess hall to see who else had arrived.

"Hey, Jessie!"

Jess cringed. Nobody had called her Jessie in years. She instantly felt her gangly, goofy younger self returning. It was like being sent back in time to when she was a teenager with braces and frizzy hair.

"Hi, Bruce." Jess walked over to the man who had called her name. Another old friend was standing next to him. "Hi, Noah."

"Good to see you, Jess," Noah said with a sheepish smile.

Jess hadn't been friends with Bruce outside of camp. He had been popular when they were teenagers, and Jess knew Ashley had crushed on him hard.

Noah had found Jess on social media a few years ago, and they talked every once in a while. Sometimes Jess hoped they would talk more, but since they lived a few states away from each other, it was difficult to do more than catch up on occasion.

"So, you coming skinny-dipping in the lake tonight?" Bruce wiggled his eyebrows.

Noah smacked his arm lightly. "You told me swimming, not skinny-dipping."

"Prude," Bruce said. "Jessie, you coming? Maybe you could bring Ashley with you."

"I'll ask her when she gets here," Jess conceded. "But we'll definitely be wearing bathing suits."

"Did you see the picture they put up of Billy? Seems like they could have found one where he actually washed his hair," Bruce said to Noah.

"Bruce, come on. Still?" Noah muttered.

"I'm just saying that they could have found one where he didn't look like a total creep. Or, on second thought, maybe that's all they had."

Jess saw the picture on the wall as she left the mess hall. "In memoriam," a plaque said under it. She thought Billy looked sweet as ever.

Bruce had always bullied Billy, the boy who had drowned, picking on him relentlessly. Jess felt a pang of grief as she looked at the picture. His face looked unbearably young, frozen forever at age sixteen.

Jess had tried not to dwell on the accident after she left camp, but she was glad Billy hadn't been forgotten entirely. She just wished Bruce would stop insulting him. It seemed cruel to bully a dead kid.

Later that night, Ashley and Jess reunited in the mess hall over dinner, and Ashley squealed in delight when Jess suggested the midnight swim. When the sun went down, the two put on bathing suits—Ashley a neon-pink bikini and Jess a trusty black one-piece—and trudged barefoot down to the lake with towels in hand.

"I feel like I'm sneaking out," Ashley said after they had tiptoed out of the cabin.

"The water is going to be freezing," Jess said.

Noah and Bruce were already sitting down with their feet dangling off the edge when Jess and Ashley got there.

"How cold is that water?" Jess asked, sitting beside Noah.

"Best plan is to just jump in," Ashley said. "That way you can't change your mind."

With that, she ditched her towel and jumped into the water

with an elegant dive. She cleared the water from her eyes when she surfaced.

"Well," she taunted while treading water, "are you all coming?"

Bruce cannonballed into the water with a running start, spraying Noah and Jess as he crashed through the surface. The water was freezing.

"Maybe I'll give it a minute before I get in," Jess said, deciding she'd hang out with Noah on the dock.

They chatted about the past while Ashley and Bruce swam.

Bruce disappeared under the surface, and with a scream Ashley went under as well.

"Very funny, Bruce," Ashley said when she resurfaced and pushed her hair back.

"It wasn't me," Bruce said with a sly smile. "It was Billy. His ghost wants you to join him."

"Ha ha, you're hilarious," Ashley said while Bruce made boo noises and splashed her.

Jess didn't like the joke. Suddenly, the lake started to feel eerie.

Bruce dove under the water again, this time grabbing Noah's ankle, which dangled over the dock. He pulled Noah into the lake. Noah came up coughing water.

"Billy got you," Bruce said.

"Come on, Bruce, that's taking it too far." Noah didn't look any more enthused about the joke than Jess was.

"Oh no! Now Billy's ghost has me!" Bruce said in a fake shrill voice, dropping under the water, acting as if his leg had been pulled.

"Cut it out," Noah said, hauling himself back up on the dock.

A wind blew past Jess, and it felt like something in the air had changed. Bruce kept up the joke, dunking himself and coughing, but suddenly his actions turned more frantic. If she didn't know any better, Jess would say it almost looked like someone was pulling Bruce under.

"Seriously, this is freaking me out." Ashley swam over to Bruce, trying and failing to keep his much larger body above the water.

She lost her hold on him, and Bruce slipped under the surface and out of her reach. Ashley started swimming, looking for him, but it was too dark to see more than a few inches in the water.

He stayed down for far too long, and Noah jumped in to help Ashley search for him. Jess grabbed the phone she had left by their towels and called for help.

It was several minutes before Bruce's body surfaced. They tried to perform CPR, and so did the medics when they arrived, but he had been under for too long.

"Drowned to death," the EMT solemnly declared. "These waters are cursed ones."

The friends were in shock, holding on to one another for support. Ashley buried her head in Jess's shoulder and cried as the medics covered the body, but not before Jess caught sight of Bruce's ankle, marked by a nasty red mark, almost as if someone had been dragging him under.

"Cursed indeed," Jess whispered.

Man's Best Friend

Dave hadn't been to his grandma's house in years. He had moved several states away about a decade ago and could only make the trek back to visit on rare occasions. When he learned he had a business meeting nearby, he rang his grandmother, Agnes, and asked if he could visit for a few days.

His grandmother had been overjoyed. She had baked dozens of cookies, prepared the guest room for him, and made a pitcher of lemonade.

"You didn't have to go to so much trouble," he said when he was sitting at the kitchen table with her, sipping lemonade and nibbling a cookie.

"It's no trouble at all," Agnes said. "I love having a reason to spruce up the place. Plus, I want to show you what I've been working on."

She walked into the living room and came back in with a massive photo album.

Agnes had decorated the pages with stickers, jewels, and sayings on every page. Dave could tell she had loved every second of making the scrapbook. She had collected photos of her children, grandchildren, siblings, and friends from every walk of life. The memories spanned years, with photos of birthdays, weddings, and little celebrations.

With each page they turned, Agnes had some kind of story to go along with the picture, and Dave found himself sitting there for well over an hour.

"Is that Grandpa?" Dave stopped on a page with a photograph of a man who looked to be in his thirties. Dave had never known his grandfather, who had died before Dave was born, but the photo looked incredibly familiar. In fact, the man in the photo looked almost exactly like Dave.

"See, I always used to say you two looked alike," Agnes said, pointing a finger at the photo. "I think so now more than ever."

The resemblance was uncanny. Dave and his grandpa could have been twins. Next to the man in the picture was a small, scruffy dog sitting politely.

"Cute dog," Dave said with a smile.

"Sandy," Agnes said, squinting at the picture. "She loved your grandpa. Followed him everywhere. She would always wait for him in the barn while he worked the farm."

"That's sweet."

"It was," Agnes said sadly. "The day he died, she was waiting for him in the barn. I could barely get her to come inside. She ran back out there every chance she got, waiting for him to come back. Poor thing was never the same without him."

"I don't think I've ever been in the barn," Dave said, curious.

"It's a bit of a mess, if I'm being honest. After your grandpa died, I sold off most of the farmland. Always said I would have someone come by and take the barn down, but I never got around to it."

"Would you mind if I went out there?"

"Sure, explore all you like. Just mind your step," Agnes said. "And wear a jacket so you don't catch a chill."

That afternoon Dave took a walk down to the barn. The old dirt pathway leading to it was nearly covered with grass and weeds, but he made his way there easily enough. Up ahead, Dave could see the half-open barn doors, faded and discolored from years of neglect. He was surprised the old thing was still standing.

As Dave approached, he heard what sounded like a happy bark in the wind.

It reminded him of Sandy, and he suddenly felt incredibly sad for her. She had waited in vain all that time for her owner.

As Dave walked up to the door, he heard the bark again.

A small, scruffy dog came running out of the barn. She sat politely at the door, head tilted, waiting. Then Dave saw the name on the tag of her collar.

Sandy.

Or, in this case, Dave thought with a shudder, *Sandy's ghost.*

Like a mirage, she seemed to fade in and out of existence as she sat there, and he approached her cautiously.

Sandy's tail wagged in a rapid rhythm as she looked at Dave lovingly, and her happy yips increased. She chased her tail in a circle, and when Dave crouched down to greet her, she jumped up, scrabbling for attention.

The recognition from Sandy was unmistakable. She must have thought Dave was his grandpa. He couldn't explain to her he wasn't the same man, but she didn't seem to care.

"Hey, girl." Dave gave her head a pat, accepting the lavish kisses from the dog and giving her a hearty belly rub when she rolled over in ecstasy.

"That's a good girl," Dave said, scratching behind Sandy's ears when she sat up again for more attention.

The joy on her face radiated. At long last, her owner had come home. With one more happy bark, Sandy's contented spirit faded away, leaving Dave alone in front of the barn.

Stopped in His Tracks

"You're telling me you haven't edited that photo at all?" Max couldn't believe the bright-blue lake waters and kelly-green trees surrounding her family's cabin. These colors looked like they belonged in a box of crayons, not the great outdoors, but Adrienne assured him it was all real.

Everything about Adrienne felt like the real deal. When Max met her at a friend's moving-away party at the start of the summer, her wit and effortless smile stopped him in his tracks. She was mesmerizing. He'd never been much of a relationship kind of guy, but when he met Adrienne, that all changed. He was hanging on her every word, and he couldn't wait to spend more time with her. Within just a few months, they were married.

When they arrived at the cabin for the first time, Max confirmed that she hadn't been lying about the lake's beauty one bit. If anything, she'd undersold it. Adrienne had grown up in this town, and she knew all the best spots in the area—namely, Lake Monyoco, which was lined with evergreen trees and boasted breezy summers perfect for getting out on the boat. Her family's cabin was situated at the northernmost end of the lake, and she'd often featured it in her hometown stories.

"Welcome to luxury!" Adrienne shouted as they unloaded groceries into the kitchen. Adrienne gave him a quick tour of the place, which felt more like a spa than a cabin. Decked out with fully renovated interiors, a hot tub, and even a private cinema room—this was sure to be a weekend to remember.

"Babe, I think the light in here is out," Max called as he unloaded their food into the fridge.

"Uh-oh," she called from the next room. "Power's out in here too."

Max scurried through the house, flipping on and off as many switches as he could find, but he had no luck.

"All our food is going to spoil."

"It's going to be fun." Adrienne came up behind Max and wrapped him in a hug, kissing the top of his shoulder. "Don't stress so much."

"Well," Max said, relaxing his shoulders, "we wanted an unplugged weekend, and we're definitely going to get it."

"Does that mean we can eat s'mores for dinner?"

Max laughed, relenting to Adrienne's endless good attitude. "Yes, but only if you know how to start a fire. I failed Eagle Scouts."

They spent the day fishing in the stream, hiking along the trails near the cabin, and playing cards by the fire. It didn't take long before they were both curled up on the patio together, full from the unreasonable amounts of chocolate and marshmallows they had just consumed, watching the sunset and trading stories. And soon, in the peacefulness of the moment, Adrienne dozed off to sleep.

Best to let her rest, Max thought as he went inside to unpack his suitcase, *before we totally lose the light for the evening.*

Unfamiliar with the space, Max treaded carefully around every corner, doing his best not to bump into anything of value. He located his suitcase in the entryway and moved down the hallway in search of a bedroom. He judiciously turned on the flashlight on his phone. He barely had any battery left, and once he ran out, that would be it until they departed two days later if the electricity didn't turn back on.

He heard a creaking floorboard farther down the hall.

"Addi?" Max could swear it sounded like footsteps.

When no one replied, Max decided to trudge ahead, keeping an ear out for any rogue animal that might have made a home here while Adrienne's family had been away.

He pushed open a door at the end of the hallway, and when he opened it, a bright fluorescent light momentarily blinded him as it lit up the entire corner of the hallway.

Instead of a bedroom, he found a closet of shoes. Not just a few pairs of shoes—floor-to-ceiling shelves filled with pairs of

loafers, flip-flops, and sneakers. Some worn, some brand-new, all different sizes, and all belonging to men.

Max slammed the door shut, although he didn't know why. He needed that light to see, but something about the fleet of shoes made him feel funny.

He stumbled into the next door he could find. He tried to use his phone's flashlight, but he couldn't get it to turn on.

As his eyes adjusted to the darkness, Max saw a man standing in the corner of the bedroom, hovering above the ground. He looked eerily similar to Max—six foot two, broad shoulders, well-dressed—except the man had no feet.

Before Max could let out a scream, the man whispered in a raspy voice, "Run."

Then he vanished.

The door behind Max swung open.

"Hey, babe." Adrienne's voice was lower. She didn't sound like herself, and she had an odd look in her eyes. "Where'd you go?" She held the s'mores skewer in her right hand and a torch from the firepit in her left.

"Just unpacking," Max sputtered, a nervous quiver in his voice. For a moment, neither of them moved, locked in a stare.

"Don't let me stop you." Adrienne smiled, still blocking the doorway.

As Max moved to try to leave, Adrienne lunged at him, her skewer jamming into his right shoulder. He shoved her away and she tripped over his suitcase and fell. He leaped toward the window overlooking the lake, then grabbed the nearest heavy object and slammed it through the glass. It would be a treacherous fall into the choppy water below, but it was the only option. That's when Adrienne let out a horrendous scream.

Max looked back to see the ghostly man restraining her. She dropped the torch and skewer as she fought him off.

"Run!" the man repeated, louder now, as flames started to spread around the room.

Max ran to the front door and up the wooded drive as the house started to burn. Max's shoulder was bleeding and his pant leg was torn, but there was no time to think.

He ran and he ran and he ran, just as the ghost urged, desperate to evade the fate of all the footless victims who had come before him.

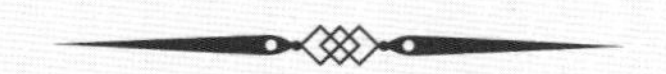

Last Call

Ivy's first shift as a bartender was off to an interesting start. She had worked as a busser and a hostess at a place down the road for several years, and she had finally worked her way up to a job at the most popular bar in town.

Brenda, the bar's longtime manager, had trained Ivy herself. Brenda had been there when Ivy arrived for her first shift, cheering her on.

"There's just one thing you've got to remember to do," Brenda said before she left Ivy on her own. "You have to put out a beer for Theo."

"Who's Theo?" Ivy asked. She didn't remember hearing anything about a regular guest during her training.

"Well, he was the owner," Brenda said. "But now he's

just our friendly ghost. As long as you leave him a beer, he's happy."

A small grin crept across Ivy's face, unsure if Brenda was serious or if this was some kind of first-night hazing tradition.

"Nothing fancy," Brenda added. "He won't want you eating into the profits. Just leave it on the end of the bar for him."

"Sure, if you say so," Ivy said, laughing off the request and giving her attention to paying customers.

Her first shift wasn't too busy since it was a weeknight, but Ivy still found herself running around in circles. By 9:00 p.m., there were only a few guests lingering at the bar.

Ivy stacked empty glasses over by the dishwasher to load up, but one fell off the bar and shattered on the ground. She thought she'd put them far enough in, but they must have been too close to the edge.

"Darn it," she muttered to herself while she got out the broom. "This is not the time to be clumsy."

When she was nearly done cleaning the glass, a second one came flying off the counter, landing on the ground and breaking into tiny shards.

Ivy was frustrated at having to start over. Moving in haste, she cut her finger on one of the jagged edges.

"Great, just what I need right now."

She called over to one of the waiters and asked him to cover the bar for her for a minute while she cleaned her dripping blood.

She put her order notebook and pen down next to the register and went to the bathroom to bandage her finger. When she came back, the notebook and pen were missing.

"Hey, did you grab my notebook?" she called over to the waiter who had covered for her. He insisted he hadn't, and Ivy continued looking for it. She eventually found the notebook on the ground in the corner of the bar, soaked in a heavy stout.

Probably a prank from the kitchen staff, she thought. Ugh, it was just the warm welcome she had been hoping for.

And then it hit her. Was Brenda serious about the ghost?

Ridiculous, she scolded herself. *That's insane.*

A few minutes later, one of the customers flagged her down.

"I'm sorry to be a pain, but this isn't what I ordered." The woman pointed to the wineglass in front of her.

Ivy remembered taking her order.

"Sauvignon blanc, right?" Ivy asked as she looked at the glass.

"Well, yes, but . . ." The woman stared down as Ivy realized the contents of the wineglass were not, in fact, wine. The glass was filled to the brim with foaming beer.

"I'm so sorry," Ivy said, snatching up the glass, embarrassed by the silly mistake. "I don't know how that happened. Let me get you a new glass."

Ivy dumped out the beer that had mysteriously appeared and poured the woman a fresh glass of wine, double-checking that the contents were correct and apologizing profusely to the guest for the mistake. The woman brushed it off, but when a second customer complained that he had been given a beer instead of water, Ivy's mind was made up.

She got out a glass and walked over to the taps. "Nothing fancy," Brenda had said, so Ivy picked the cheapest beer they had and poured a full glass. Then she went over and placed it on the end of the bar, cursing herself for caving.

Whether it made Theo happy, she couldn't say, but no more customers complained about getting the wrong drink. No more broken glasses. And her notebook stayed put for the rest of her shift.

At the end of the night, when she went to clean up the drink she had left out for Theo, the glass was empty.

Christmas Past

Cece had found the old portrait buried in the attic a few weeks ago and decided it was the perfect gift for Aunt Amelia. She was surprised she hadn't seen it before. There were so few family photos taken together of Vivian, her grandmother; Amelia, her great-aunt; and Jonas, her great-uncle. Cece had seen photos of Vivian and Amelia together, but she couldn't remember ever seeing all three siblings in one image. This portrait was of the three of them as young adults.

Each of the siblings was smiling happily. Vivian sat in an armchair in the center of the portrait, with Amelia and Jonas framing her on either side like small Renaissance statues.

The portrait likely once hung in her great-grandparents' home, but it had long since been buried in Cece's father's attic, tossed in with other old family heirlooms he had collected over the years. It had been her father's idea to have the portrait reframed for Aunt Amelia, the only remaining sibling.

Vivian had died shortly after giving birth to Cece's father, and Jonas was a bit of a family mystery. Nobody spoke of him.

Amelia had moved into an assisted living facility earlier in the year, and Cece knew she was feeling lonely. She hoped having the portrait would help cheer up her aunt.

"Merry Christmas!" Cece yelled into Amelia's apartment as she hauled the large portrait that she'd carefully wrapped into the living room. Amelia took her time coming out of the bedroom, pushing her new walker in front of her.

She had complained fiercely when she first got the walker, but Cece knew that her aunt was secretly pleased for the small amount of independence it gave her.

"Well, isn't this an awful lot of fuss?"

Amelia sat down in her favorite chair while Cece propped the wrapped portrait up against a wall.

"There's no such thing as too much fuss for you, Auntie." Cece gave her beloved aunt a kiss on the cheek. Amelia never married or had any children, but she had doted on Cece as if she were her grandmother.

"What's all that?" Amelia pointed to the portrait.

"It's your Christmas present!" Cece said excitedly. "Do you want to see?"

Amelia asked Cece to unveil the gift for her, and Cece dutifully ripped off the wrapping paper.

Cece stared at the painting in confusion.

There was nobody sitting in the chair. Vivian was gone.

"I don't understand," Cece said, stepping closer to the painting. "I swear this is the same portrait, but I thought it had all three of you."

Confused and concerned, she looked toward Amelia and noticed that the old woman was weeping silently. Cece crouched down in front of her and took one of her hands, but Amelia shook her off and stood up.

"There's something I need to show you," Amelia said as she pulled out a stack of photos from a drawer and handed them to Cece.

The top photo looked familiar, and Cece could swear it was one she had seen before. But the version she remembered had both Vivian and Amelia, and this one just had Amelia.

"It's been happening for years." Amelia pointed at the empty spot where Vivian should have been in the picture, then turned toward the portrait. "She refuses to be in a picture with me. Not while I've kept his secret."

"What do you mean?" Cece asked, disoriented and unnerved by what she was seeing.

"It was all my fault." Amelia wept. "I didn't want him to get in trouble, but I shouldn't have protected him."

"Are you talking about Jonas?" Cece asked, sitting on the couch opposite her aunt. "You always told me he was a jerk who abandoned the family, but that's not exactly a secret."

"No." Amelia shook her head. "I told you that so you wouldn't ask questions, but the truth is much worse."

Amelia sighed, wiping her tears and sniffling.

"Jonas was indeed a jerk. He was also a thief . . . But the worst of it was . . ." Amelia couldn't bring herself to say the words.

"What?" Cece said softly.

"One time, after Jonas went on a spree, repeatedly burgling our father, Vivian threatened to turn him in to the police. I heard them yelling out back at Jonas's house on the porch, their voices raised. And then I heard a large thud," Amelia whispered, her whole body shaking as she recounted the events.

"The screaming stopped, and only one of them came back inside. I knew . . ." Amelia confessed. "But I protected him. I lied for him so he wouldn't be charged. I lied so he wouldn't come for me . . ."

"Oh, Auntie." Cece reached out for Amelia's bony hand. "That's not your fault."

"She was my sister. My best friend." Amelia shook her head. "And I let her murderer get away with it. I was afraid. Carrying the burden of that secret has haunted me for years. I thought it would be better if it died with me. But perhaps it's time for the truth to be known so Vivian can finally rest in peace."

Cece got up and hugged her aunt, unable to imagine the scope of her pain.

When Amelia looked back at the portrait, Vivian sat in the chair beside her sister once again, smiling out at them.

All Aboard

Great, Kira thought. Exactly what she needed right now. Her car wouldn't start. It had sputtered and coughed suddenly, with the fuel light flashing, before it died completely. She thought she still had at least half a tank of gas, so she was surprised when her car just stopped running, leaving her in the middle of the train tracks.

Despite her best efforts, she couldn't get it to start again. The empty fuel light flashed at her mockingly. She would have to call for a tow truck.

Being stopped directly over the train tracks made Kira uncomfortable. It wasn't the safest spot to be by any means. Barring pushing her car a few feet away via some Herculean strength, it wasn't going to budge.

She thought about waiting outside the car, but it was the middle of winter, and the idea of standing out in the cold was less than appealing. The tow truck had said it would be half an hour before it got there.

Cursing herself for getting into this situation, she pulled out her phone again. If she was going to be stuck here for a little while, she should at least check the train schedule. It would ease her mind to know nothing was coming by.

Kira searched the internet for her location, the train line, and the current time. According to her research, there weren't any scheduled trains for at least another hour.

Good, she thought, *no immediate danger.* Then she heard a faint noise in the wind, although she couldn't quite put her finger on it. She rolled down her window and heard a small hum, sounding almost human. She closed the window, but the humming persisted. *This will be a long half-hour wait*, Kira thought.

Kira continued to scroll, trying to redirect her thoughts and stay calm. An article on the search page caught her eye. The headline read, "Fatal Railroad Accident on Main Street."

A bit morbid, Kira thought, but she had time to kill, so she clicked on the article. It was from about five years ago and detailed how a man's car had been hit when he got stuck on the tracks. Right where she was now.

A shiver went down her spine. Even the date was the same, January 12, *exactly* five years ago.

The article stated the man's car had been hit at 9:22 p.m.

She looked at the clock. It was currently 9:21 p.m.

Fear made the hair on the back of her neck stand up.

As the clock turned to 9:22 p.m., she heard the blare of a train horn to her right. She turned and was nearly blinded by bright, rapidly approaching headlights.

She had been wrong. There was a train, and it was coming right at her.

Kira hit the gas pedal pointlessly, then fumbled for the door handle.

She tried to push the door open, but every time she unlocked it, the button pressed down and the door locked shut.

Panic overtook her. The train was still barreling in her direction, mere seconds away now. She wondered if this was how the man from the article had felt before he died. Helpless.

Kira heard the sound of the train's wheels on the tracks and the dinging of the crossing gate as the train got closer. There was no possibility she would be able to get out of the way in time.

She braced herself for the impact as the train raced toward her, closing her eyes tight and gripping the wheel.

The train was three seconds away.

Two.

One.

Kira screamed as the train collided with the passenger door, but her car didn't so much as twitch at the impact. The sounds of the train silenced, and when she opened her eyes, the train was gone. Any trace of it had vanished into a thick mist that was now surrounding the car.

She looked at the clock. 9:23 p.m.

Kira heard the sound of humming once again and tried to

steady her shaking hands. She couldn't stay on this train track. She would go insane. Or die.

Giving one last desperate attempt, she turned on the car. It whirred to life, and the gas tank showed it was half full.

No empty fuel light.

She slammed her foot down on the gas pedal, and the car drove forward with a lurch, showing no sign it had been dead and immovable just moments before.

Kira drove away shaking, driving a bit faster than usual. As she left the train tracks behind, the sound of a man humming radiated in the night.

Play Me a Song

Florence thought the house was far too quiet. Roy had wanted a fresh start after returning from the war and had purchased the house on a secluded plot of land on a whim. *A piano would help*, Florence thought. *Maybe a dog.* They dreamed of the days when they would have a few kids running around. Happy noise, happy home.

When she found the record player in the attic, covered in dust, it had seemed like a sign. Music would cheer the whole place right up. There was only one album, an old, dusty thing Florence had never heard before, but she didn't mind one bit.

She set up the record player in the middle of the living room before they even had any furniture and played that one record on repeat while they moved in.

"Can't you play something else?" Roy had complained after the fifth time through the same record.

"I'll look for some new albums next time I'm in town," Florence had replied. For now, this record suited her just fine. It was much better than the quiet. It didn't take long for Florence to learn every word to every song on the record, and she found herself singing or humming the tunes even when the record player wasn't on.

For Christmas that year, Roy bought Florence a whole box of records. There was something from every genre, and Florence played them all, dancing in the living room and dragging Roy in twirling circles with her.

Even when her record collection had dozens of options, Florence's favorite was still that first album. Whether she was blissfully happy or overwhelmingly sad, it was always the first thing she reached for when she wanted to listen to something that felt like home.

The children Florence had hoped would fill their home never came, and the dog died, and then a cat, and even a pet bird who used to squeak gleefully from its cage.

But Roy and Florence lived happily in the house for many years, filling it with noise and music. When pneumonia overcame Florence one brutal winter, she grew so sick she couldn't get out of bed.

"Roy," she had asked, propped up by pillows, "will you play me a song?"

Roy had lugged the old record player into the bedroom and put on Florence's favorite album. The music and Roy's voice were the last things she heard as she died.

With Florence gone, the house felt emptier and quieter than ever. Roy felt purposeless, as if all the joyful noise had left his life along with Florence.

From upstairs, the record player that he had never brought back down started playing on its own. Florence's favorite record. Despite his sadness, Roy smiled to himself, feeling less alone with his wife's favorite songs to comfort him.

When Roy himself died many years later, the house was sold, and a family with three young children moved in. They were rowdy, joyful, and, best of all, loud. The house was filled with noise again as they moved in, lugging boxes and setting up furniture.

Brandon and Elsie, the new owners of the house, planned to clean out the attic where the Realtor had stored some of Roy's belongings. So while Elsie brought in the last of their boxes, Brandon climbed up the rickety stairs.

Most of the items up here are getting tossed, Brandon thought as he looked around. *Better not let the kids see the birdcage that's up here or they'll be begging for a new pet.*

In the corner was a record player, clearly well-loved but broken. Brandon mentally slated that for the trash as well. Maybe he would keep some of the records though. It was an awesome collection.

As he sorted through the relics, he wondered what Roy had been like. The Realtor said he was an older man who had passed away, and Brandon thought it was sad that he hadn't had any family come to reclaim these last belongings.

The old man must have been lonely. Brandon couldn't imagine being in a house this big without Elsie. And his kids could be a pain sometimes, but he loved them more than anything.

From the corner of the attic, the record player started turning. Surprised, Brandon listened as an old album played. He hadn't thought the record player would work, and he hadn't turned it on. The song only played for a minute, and Brandon wrote it off as a quirk of an old machine.

He tried playing another album on the record player, but for some reason, the songs remained the same. He removed the record, but it didn't seem to matter. Music continued to play.

Unnerved, he grabbed the record player and barreled down the attic stairs, rushing out the front door past his wife. He lumbered to the edge of the driveway, depositing the record player a good quarter mile away from the house, praying that someone would pick it up and take it off his hands.

Sweaty, he returned inside, but the music was still there.

"Elsie?" he called. "Do you hear that?"

"Dad, try this!" Brandon's son, Matthew, exclaimed, whirring around the corner and practically tripping over himself in excitement. He held out a plate of peach pie, still steaming from the oven.

"You're supposed to be unpacking. Where did you get that?"

"Oh, Roy, dear," a voice called from around the corner. He didn't know whose voice it was, but it wasn't Elsie's.

"Get back," Brandon whispered to Matthew.

Brandon approached the kitchen to find a beautiful

woman cooking at the stove, her apron perfectly arranged and curlers still in her hair.

"Oh, darling, it's been ages since I've heard that beautiful song." Her eyes shone an eerie green, and she clutched a nine-inch knife dripping in peach juice in her right hand.

"Fancy a dance?"

The Show Must Go On

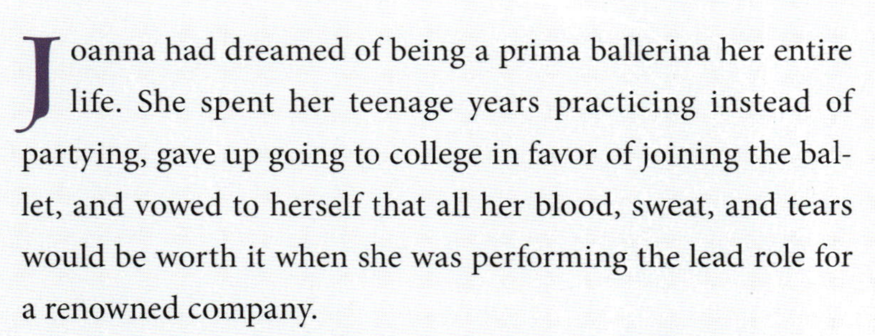

Joanna had dreamed of being a prima ballerina her entire life. She spent her teenage years practicing instead of partying, gave up going to college in favor of joining the ballet, and vowed to herself that all her blood, sweat, and tears would be worth it when she was performing the lead role for a renowned company.

Joanna's big break finally arrived when, at the age of twenty-three, she was given the starring role in her company's production of *The Sleeping Beauty.* Joanna had been overjoyed, telling everyone who would listen about the show.

So it was an absolute tragedy when Joanna died just one week before opening night. All the performers were broken-hearted, but the owner of the cash-strapped theater insisted the show must go on. Matthew, who had been Joanna's dancing partner, begged the company director to postpone. He said it wouldn't be right for them to carry on as if nothing had happened.

"She would want you to keep dancing," Evelyn, the director, insisted. "And there is an understudy waiting for her big break. Would you want to rob her of that?"

Alas, there was little to be done.

With just a few days left before opening night, Joanna's understudy, Madeline, jumped into rehearsals.

"I know it's a lot of pressure," Matthew said, "but just try to stay calm."

"Everyone expects me to be thrilled," Madeline said with concern. "I'm so lucky. That's what my teachers said when I told them. But I just feel gross."

Matthew couldn't help but agree. Nothing about this situation felt lucky at all.

At the final fitting for their costumes, Matthew watched as the costume designer brought out the tutu for Madeline to wear. It had been Joanna's costume, lovingly made by the costume designer and covered with hundreds of tiny crystals.

When they took the tutu out of the bag, they saw the costume was in shreds. Pieces of it hung at all angles, as if someone had ripped it apart or attacked it with a pair of scissors.

"I don't understand how this happened." The costume designer looked horrified at the state of her precious design.

"This has been in my home the whole time. I never let it out of my sight."

"It's all right," Madeline comforted her. "We can repurpose one of my old costumes. It won't be as stunning, but I'm sure it will work just fine."

The costume designer didn't seem convinced, but with so little time, she had no choice but to agree.

The night before the show, the whole ballet company gathered at the theater to do a final dress rehearsal on the stage.

The stage had been made to look like a ballroom, filled with staircases, balconies, and doorways. It was all covered with yards of flowing flower garlands.

"Joanna would have loved this," Matthew said to himself as he took in the spectacular stage design.

He waited for Madeline to join him onstage to rehearse their dance together. When they were finished, Matthew moved to the wings and watched while Madeline ran through her solo dance.

As Madeline leapt and turned across the stage, one of the set staircases began to wobble. Just as Madeline danced next to it, the staircase came crashing down, shattering into a pile of debris at Madeline's feet.

She screamed as she jumped out of the way of the falling set. It had barely missed landing right on top of her.

The whole cast was in shock. Evelyn declared dress rehearsal over for the night, demanding that the stage crew stay to fix the set before tomorrow's show.

Matthew was the last to leave, and he looked solemnly around the theater. A lone light had been left on the stage. A ghost light is a theater tradition that ensures no lingering crew would hurt themselves in the dark.

The next night Matthew and Madeline waited in the wings for the orchestra to begin playing. Matthew was excited to perform, but he still felt uncomfortable doing the show without Joanna. It felt like a betrayal to Joanna for him to live out her dream with someone else.

As Matthew and Madeline stepped on the stage, he thought that it should have been Joanna with him.

Their duet ended with an impressive lift, Madeline over Matthew's head, defying gravity. As he lifted her up, Matthew noticed a shift in the lights.

That isn't supposed to happen, he thought. *The lights are supposed to dim, not get brighter.* Suddenly, the spotlight swiveled, pointing directly into Matthew's eyes.

He tried to lower Madeline down gracefully so she could carry on with her solo, but the blinding light made him misjudge the distance to the floor. Madeline was much shorter than Joanna was, and Matthew dropped just a moment too early. She fell several inches to the stage, rolling her ankle and crumbling to the ground with a sickening thud.

The crowd gasped as Madeline fell, and Matthew bent down to help her as panic swept over him.

"Are you hurt?" he asked her as the orchestra fumbled. Madeline clutched her ankle, her face in agony.

"I think it's broken." Tears slipped down Madeline's face.

Matthew gestured at the stage crew to close the curtain, leaving a bemused audience on the other side.

There was no way Madeline would be able to finish the

performance. She was rushed to the hospital, and Evelyn dismissed the audience, promising them free tickets to an upcoming performance.

The company packed up their belongings and went home for the night, weary and unsure how they would proceed the next morning.

Matthew waited while everyone left the theater, sitting in the last row of seats in shock. And as he did, he watched as a shadow crossed over the ghost light on the stage. It swirled across the light, moving around the stage in utter silence. The tip of her head, the angle of her arabesque—he knew that dancer.

It was Joanna, dancing in her lead role at last.

Picture Perfect

Do you ever stop taking pictures, Cleo?" Jason asked. He was pretty sure she had taken fifteen pictures in the last five minutes.

"Nope." Cleo smiled, snapping another selfie. "Gotta make sure I get the right one for socials. Not too posed, but still showing off how cool this is."

"I don't think anyone is looking at the background when you're in the pic, babe," Logan said, draping an arm over Cleo's shoulder.

The hike they were on had been an excuse for a double date with Jason and Logan's friend Jenn. Cleo and Logan had been begging Jason and Jenn to go out with each other for weeks now. Dating apps had led Jason to nothing but losers recently, and he needed a new way to meet people. Cleo had insisted he and Jenn would be perfect together, and even though Jason didn't love the idea of a blind date, he had finally agreed.

Cleo was right. Jenn was adorable, and so far, she and Jason had been getting along really well.

The hike was a fairly easy one, just a three-mile loop with lots of well-traveled trails and tourist-trap photo spots. The day was nice enough that the trails were busy, and they passed other groups every few minutes as they walked.

Logan walked a bit faster than the rest, making his way up the path and around a bend.

"You guys have got to see this!" he shouted back at them. Cleo took off at a light jog, but Jason and Jenn kept their pace the same.

As they rounded the bend, Jason noticed a memorial marker for someone named Alex that had been placed at the top of the outlook. The memorial looked fairly new, and Jason thought he remembered a recent news story about someone trying to take a selfie at the edge and falling off the cliff.

Jason could see why people would want pictures of this. The view over the river was incredible, and the hill they were on jutted out into a sharp and imposing cliff.

Someone from the park's service had put up barriers at the edge of the cliff with signs saying, "Authorized Personnel Only."

Cleo took out her camera again, capturing the amazing views.

"These barriers are hideous," she said, adjusting her lens

to try to cut them out of the frame. "Did they have to pick orange?"

Jason thought the view was still nice, even if it wasn't the perfect photo spot, but Cleo didn't seem pleased with how any of her angles were turning out.

She walked up to the barriers, looked around to make sure nobody was watching them, then swung a leg over one.

"Are you insane?" Jason asked. "They wouldn't have put those there if it was safe to be that close to the edge."

"I'm sure it's fine," Logan said, joining Cleo on the other side. "They're probably just here to keep idiots from tripping and falling into the river."

"And you're not idiots?" Jenn joked.

"Come on. Let's get one selfie together," Cleo pleaded. "It'll just take two seconds."

Jason and Jenn hesitated but eventually caved to Cleo's demands. They tentatively climbed over the barrier and stood next to Cleo and Logan.

"Say cheese," Cleo said with a smile as she took the picture.

As they moved to climb back over the barrier, the rocks shifted beneath their feet. A few pebbles broke off and clattered over the edge of the cliff, scattering into the river below. Then a larger chunk broke, causing them all to lose their footing.

Cleo tripped, lifting her camera up into the air to keep it from breaking. Jenn and Logan toppled into each other, landing in a heap on the ground.

But Jason slipped, his foot going over the edge. He flailed his arms out to the side, flapping them wildly and trying to regain his balance. He was sure he was going to fall right off

the cliff. *Serves me right for going over the barriers,* he thought. *I'll be the next one with a memorial marker.*

Suddenly, Jason felt a tug on the front of his shirt, yanking him back up. As he steadied himself on the edge, he looked around, but he couldn't figure out who had grabbed him.

When they had climbed back over the barriers and were sitting on the ground catching their breath, Logan tried to lighten the mood. "At least we got a good picture. Let's see it, Cleo."

She took out her camera and pulled up the picture. It was good, Jason thought. The background was definitely pretty.

But he was shocked to see a blurry figure of a fifth person standing directly beside him on the cliff edge.

Lost and Found

Emma had been missing for forty-eight hours now. Her friends and family were frantic. It wasn't like her to go so long without checking in. Her parents, Annie and Fred, had always praised her independence, and even though Emma lived on her own and often traveled alone, she always talked to someone daily. Just to be safe.

Emma's travels were inspired by her mother's mother, Delilah, who first caught the travel bug the summer of her sophomore year with little idea of where she was headed. These monthslong summer adventures became a lifelong tradition for Delilah, taking her far and wide around the world. As a little girl, Emma used to love curling up in Delilah's lap, hearing about the mountains of Nepal or the long train rides through Eastern Europe. She also loved the small collection of coins her grandmother brought back for her, and she'd kept them in a small box on her bedside table. At Delilah's funeral, people flocked from all over the world to pay their respects to their dear friend, and Emma couldn't believe how many people knew and loved her grandmother.

Emma wanted to live a life like that.

But now the police had officially declared her missing. They had begun a search, starting with locations she frequented, looking for leads.

Annie had a spare key to Emma's apartment, so she and Fred went over to see if anything indicated where their daughter had gone. They didn't even know if she was in the country or not.

Emma had always been impeccably tidy, so Annie wasn't surprised that nothing looked out of place. She sat down on the couch to gather her thoughts.

"Think like Emma," she said to herself, closing her eyes.

Fred shuffled through several pieces of mail on Emma's bedside table, looking for clues. But all he found were a few receipts, concert tickets, and a box of old coins.

Annie's phone buzzed multiple times in succession in her pocket, a sign of texts coming in. Her mouth dropped open in shock.

Delilah had sent her three texts, each containing a single letter.

F

I

N

Annie waited anxiously, watching as Delilah typed.

D

Annie could hardly believe what she was reading.

"Fred, you need to see this."

Fred joined her on the couch, and another letter came through.

H

E

Annie started typing frantically, desperate for answers. But when she hit send on the message, it failed.

One last text came in from Delilah: *R*.

Find her.

"I'm trying!" Annie shouted.

She attempted to text Delilah again, but once again it failed to send. Annie tried to call, but it went straight to voicemail.

No more texts came through.

The radio on Emma's nightstand suddenly turned on, rapidly cycling through staticky stations. At first, nothing was clear, but then one word came through clear as day: "Briar."

When she was a little girl, Emma loved hiking in Briar Woods. The whole family used to go on camping trips there, and it was a highlight for Emma every summer. But their family had moved several states away and hadn't been back in years. Could that be where Emma had gone?

Shaken and confused, Annie and Fred hopped in the car, plugged in the address, and headed west as fast as they could. They advised the police to send a rescue unit to the woods, which spanned miles and miles of land. It could be a long search, and they didn't want to lose any time.

As Fred drove, Annie scrolled through old photos and videos of Emma, tears blurring her eyes. She hit play on one of the videos. It was a birthday message Emma had sent to Annie. Emma had been traveling this year, so she had sent the short clip.

"Happy birthday, Mom!" Emma's voice rang out through the phone. "Love you lots and can't wait to celebrate with you soon. Cheers!"

The video left Annie crying, but seeing Emma's face was comforting.

She hit play again.

"Happy birthday, Mom! Love you . . ." The image on the screen crackled, and suddenly it was no longer Emma in the frame but rather Annie's long-deceased mother, Delilah. Her face was serious but calm.

"Elm Brook Trail."

Annie was overwhelmed to hear her mom's voice again after all these years. In shock, she dropped the phone while the rest of the message played. She scrambled to pick it up again, hitting play to start it over, but this time the video was the same as it had always been. Just a birthday message from Emma—nothing odd about it.

Fred and Annie drove ahead in disbelief.

Annie again called the police to advise they check the Elm Brook Trail at Briar Woods.

"Any particular reason you think she would have gone there?" one of the police officers asked.

"Just a feeling," Annie said warily, not wanting to admit that she thought the ghost of her mother was somehow sending her clues. "She always liked that trail."

A few hours later, teary and frantic, Annie and Fred finally arrived at Briar Woods.

A host of police cars were parked in the lot, and the officers explained to Annie and Fred that they had a rescue crew up and down the trail. They'd alert them immediately if they found Emma and advised them to find a hotel for the night.

Of course, Annie and Fred wouldn't accept that answer. They were going to go into those woods to find their daughter, and no one would tell them otherwise.

"Mom? Dad?" From the trail, a hopeful voice squeaked out.

Fred and Annie wept. There was Emma, emerging from a row of elm trees, hobbling with a swollen ankle. Her parents rushed over to embrace her as a swell of emotions rose within them.

"You'll never guess who helped me find my way out." Emma could barely speak.

She placed a small coin in her mother's hand.

"I think we might," Annie said as she held her daughter tight.

The Final Shot

As the town sign for Stonefield came into view, Yasmin thought that a harsh breeze would be enough to blow it over. The posts looked like they were barely in the ground, and the sign itself seemed to be hanging on with nothing but spiderwebs.

What else would she have expected from a ghost town?

The side trip to the old mining town had seemed entertaining enough. She and Elliot had been in the car for five hours now, driving down the coast to spend the holiday celebrating the wedding of her best friend, Isabella, and they needed to stretch their legs. Elliot had been thrilled by the suggestion to learn more about the local legend and was eager to talk about anything other than the bride and groom and flowers and *relationships.* He gleefully pulled off the highway for the excursion.

As they drove through the town, Yasmin admitted that it was eerier than she had anticipated.

"I guess we don't have to worry about locking the car," Elliot joked as he parked on the side of the road. "Do you think we can go into any of these buildings?"

"I don't know," Yasmin said as she got out. "If some of the public ones are open, it's probably okay."

Elliot beamed and walked quickly up to the doors of what looked like an old saloon. They opened easily. The whole place was covered in a thick layer of dust and smelled like mildew.

"Think we should carve our names?" Elliot pointed to the wooden bar top, where countless past visitors had left their initials encircled in hearts.

"Oh, *now* you're ready to go on the record with our relationship?" Yasmin quipped. She leaned against the bar until it crumbled beneath her. "I guess we'll have to hold that thought."

"We could take a souvenir," he suggested, waving a dust-covered bottle of whiskey in the air. It still had one last shot of liquor at the bottom of the bottle.

"Absolutely not." Yasmin shook her head violently. "Put that thing down. In fact, don't touch anything else."

"Don't be such a stick in the mud. Let's have a toast to the future."

"I don't want to take anything from here." Yasmin swallowed. "It just feels ick."

As they left the bar, Yasmin was overcome by the feeling

that someone was watching them. She turned, but no one was there.

They got back on the road, but they had only driven a few miles before they heard a loud and violent pop. Elliot pulled over to the side of the road, and sure enough, a gaping hole had appeared in the side of the tire.

"Where's the spare?" Elliot asked upon opening the trunk.

"What do you mean? It should be there."

"Wooo," he mocked in his best spooky voice. "Maybe the ghosts stole it."

Yasmin let out a few choice words under her breath as she dialed for assistance. It took over an hour for anyone to arrive, which was plenty of time for Yasmin and Elliot to stew in silence and properly sweat through their clothes under the hot summer sun.

In just a few short, miserable hours, Yasmin and Elliot arrived at the rehearsal dinner, hungry from the extended drive and ready for a good meal. Yasmin, the only single one in the group, was eager to introduce Elliot to the other bridesmaids, but when they sat down at the table, there were only a few guests.

"Seems like the fish from lunch got 'em," the father of the groom whispered. "Most everyone has retired to the washrooms. Even the bride and groom, poor things."

Pale and feverish after throwing up, the bridal party dissipated for the evening, vowing to start fresh in the morning.

After breakfast the next day, Yasmin and the other bridesmaids congregated with Isabella in a room at the church, tired but determined to make the bride's day as special as it could be. Isabella's mother was running late, but no one paid much attention to that. In fact, her lateness was a bit of a gift since the bride was busy putting in some extra time with her makeup artist, still trying to cover up the puffiness under her eyes.

But as the hours passed, it became clear something had gone wrong. Isabella called her mom, with no response. Again and again, her calls were sent straight to voicemail. Tears welled in her eyes. Everyone feared something bad had happened to her.

"Everybody out!" the preacher shouted from the doorway, smoke beginning to billow from behind him.

Yasmin watched in horror as she saw ravaging flames consuming the hallway and spilling into their bridal suite. Before the girls even had a chance to gather their things, a small flame caught on a hairspray bottle, causing an explosion. Everyone spilled from the building, screaming, coughing, and stumbling in the thick, black smoke. A fire truck arrived, sirens blaring, but not before over half the church was consumed in the flames, the iron steeple crashing violently to the ground.

After consoling Isabella, Yasmin rushed to find Elliot, who was frantically searching for her in the group of people who had escaped. After a long embrace and some feeble attempts to comprehend what had caused the blaze, and after making sure everyone was okay, they decided it was best to return to the hotel, get a good night's rest, and prepare for the long journey back.

"Here, you look like you could use this," Elliot said in the car before they drove away.

He opened up the glove compartment and pulled out the whiskey bottle with its one last shot swirling in the bottom. Yasmin refused to touch it.

"You have to take it back," she demanded.

"Are you out of your mind?" He laughed.

"What if that's the reason everything has been going wrong? You ruined my best friend's wedding!"

"You're being ridiculous," Elliot huffed, rolling his eyes. "You know what? Fine." He defiantly drank the last shot.

By the time they made it to the motel, they had reached a stalemate. He wouldn't take the bottle back, and she no longer wanted to date him if he kept it.

Yasmin slammed the door to her room, and Elliot took off for a drive to cool his head.

As the police officer pulled up to the scene of the accident, he saw the wrecked car slammed up against a telephone pole and the ambulance with its whirring lights right next to it.

The EMT told him that the driver, a man named Elliot, had been dead when the ambulance pulled up. The cop looked around the scene of the accident, opening up the doors of the car. On the passenger seat sat an empty whiskey bottle.

Hide-and-Seek

Summer rolled in and school let out at last, but Jayden and Kai found themselves instantly bored. At thirteen, they were often bored, but they quickly found a way to entertain themselves. Every day they biked to the woods at the edge of town and explored.

Some days they ended up skipping rocks in streams or ponds. Other days they climbed up rock ledges or trees, racing to see who could get higher.

"Want to play manhunt?" Jayden suggested one afternoon.

"How are we going to play manhunt with two of us?" Kai said. "Isn't that just hide-and-seek?"

Jayden blushed, and he seemed embarrassed. "Yeah, I guess it's kind of dumb."

Boredom had overtaken Kai, and even though he felt like he was too old for hide-and-seek, the idea of looking for a hiding place in the woods did seem cool.

"Could be kind of fun," Kai said with a shrug. "As long as I can hide first."

Jayden grumbled about seeking first but ultimately agreed. They decided Jayden should wait two minutes before he started searching, so they set a timer on Jayden's phone. Kai took off at a jog, trying to make his footsteps light so Jayden wouldn't know which direction he had gone.

Kai started out on a path that he and Jayden had explored dozens of times before. He didn't want to be too obvious, but he also didn't want to get totally lost. Two minutes wasn't very long, and he knew he wouldn't have a lot of time to find a hiding spot. When he got to the stream, he jumped over it, looking for a path on the opposite bank.

They hadn't explored this area yet, and Kai was excited to see what he would discover.

He walked down a bramble-covered pathway to a small, fenced-in cemetery. *So cool*, he thought, opening the gate and walking through.

Kai was pretty sure Jayden would be too scared to look for him here, so he set out in search of a good hiding place. It was eerie seeing all the old, overgrown graves. *These people must be ancient*, Kai thought. It didn't look like anyone had been to this cemetery in ages.

He wished he had brought a sweatshirt as he walked through the cemetery. It had seemed warm out earlier when he left the house, but it was a lot colder now, and a chill ran through him.

Toward the back of the cemetery, a larger headstone called to Kai. He could definitely hide behind that one if he crouched down.

Sitting down on the cold ground, Kai looked around at all the graves. Most of them had the same family name, and a bunch of the dates were from the 1800s.

He heard what sounded like footsteps approaching and was disappointed Jayden had found him so easily. But if he was going to be found, he might as well do it in style. He jumped up, ready to shout at Jayden and hopefully give him a scare.

No Jayden. Looking around, Kai could see that there was nobody else in the cemetery. *Just the wind*, Kai decided, sitting back down to wait.

"Kai!" a shout came from out in the woods. Kai ducked his head. Jayden was looking for him now. Kai bet it would take at least half an hour for Jayden to figure out where he had gone. He giggled to himself as he heard Jayden shout, "Come out, Kai!"

But his laughter quickly turned to concern as he heard Jayden yell, "Kai, help!"

Kai stood up, looking in every direction to figure out where his friend's voice had come from. It could be a trick to get him to reveal his hiding spot.

"Kai, I'm hurt!" Jayden shouted. "Help!"

Kai took off from the cemetery at a run. When he made it to the stream, he heard Jayden shout from behind him, and Kai turned around, thinking he had gone in the wrong direction.

He raced back to the cemetery, but Jayden's voice was

coming from somewhere else now. Kai couldn't figure out where to go.

Taking out his phone, Kai called Jayden. It would ruin the game, but if Jayden was hurt, Kai didn't care about some dumb game.

"Bored of hiding already?" Jayden joked when he answered the phone.

Kai breathed a sigh of relief hearing Jayden's voice. He definitely wasn't hurt, and Kai was glad he was okay, even if he was a little annoyed at being manipulated into giving up.

"Not fair with the calling for help," Kai said crankily.

"What are you talking about?" Jayden said.

"Don't play dumb. You only shouted for help to get me out of hiding. You really scared me. I thought you were hurt."

"I don't know what you are talking about," Jayden said slowly. "I didn't call for you."

From a few feet away, Kai heard a voice that sounded exactly like Jayden's. "Kai, I need you."

"What was that?" Jayden asked through the phone, but Kai didn't answer. He started running as fast as he could away from the cemetery.

Curse of the North

Hunter couldn't wait to have a sleepover at his cousin Gabe's house. Hunter's parents were going away for the weekend for a wedding that sounded awfully boring to him. He had been beyond excited when his parents had said he could stay at Gabe's instead of going with them.

Gabe lived in a big old house that Hunter loved looking around in. There were lots of weird objects that were fascinating to Hunter's nine-year-old brain, and he peppered his aunt with a million "what's that?" questions every time he came to visit. Old cuckoo clocks, porcelain dolls, an ancient set of maracas, and a tall *djembe* drum—all collected from his aunt's travels around the world.

Hunter thought these antiques were way more interesting than the junk his parents decorated their house with. He wanted to travel, but his parents wouldn't take him. They told him he could go when he got older, but he was nearly ten now. He couldn't stand to wait much longer.

His favorite of his aunt's trinkets today was a display of old ceramic animal figurines she'd obtained on her travels near the North Pole from a community of vagabonds living off the land. His aunt had lined them up on the kitchen counter like a little army, one next to the other in a straight line. A few of them had little chips or scratched paint, but for the most part, they were in pretty good shape.

Most of them were Alaskan animals of some kind, and his aunt detailed to Hunter how she was fixing them all up to make them look brand-new. There was a large hawk with a chipped beak, a bear that had somehow gained a giant red spot on its back, a wolf with blue fangs, and a whale that Hunter thought looked like something out of a nightmare with its beady little eyes. A caribou with spiked horns rounded out the bunch.

Hunter always did the right thing, but for some reason, he had an intense desire to pocket one. Would she notice if he took just one? He slipped one of the figurines into his jacket when his aunt's back was turned and sauntered back to the bedroom to store the figurine in his suitcase.

That night, Hunter and Gabe set up sleeping bags on the floor, camping-style, and Hunter got inside his and drew it up to his chin before he turned out the light. Somehow the dark felt a little darker than it did in his own room at home. When he looked around the room, everything was unfamiliar, and the shadows gave it an eerie feeling.

Hunter finally dozed off after a few hours of racing thoughts, but it was not long before he was awoken by the sound of squawking at the door. Hunter opened his eyes and sat up. He didn't know Gabe had a bird.

"Hey, little birdie," he whispered into the dark to the shadow that was hovering in the crack in the door. He wasn't sure whether the bird heard him, but it whisked away down the hall, and Hunter put his head down to go back to sleep.

Later that night, he was awoken once again, this time by the feeling that something was standing on his feet. The light in the hallway had been shut off, and it was hard for Hunter to see in the dark, but a shadow of what looked like two large wings hovered over his legs. Then the bird swooped to the top of the nightstand and perched above him.

"Great, glad you're comfy," Hunter grumbled to his new friend as he drifted off.

Hunter was annoyed when he was awoken for a third time, this time by the sound of a beak pecking at the dresser. He opened his eyes to shoo the giant bird away so he could finally get some sleep, but he didn't see anything there.

Hoping it had flown off and would finally leave him alone, Hunter went back to sleep.

"How come you never told me you have a bird?" Hunter asked Gabe the next morning while they were playing a video game.

"Because we don't," Gabe said.

"Yeah, you do," Hunter insisted. "It kept bugging me last night."

"I'm not messing with you." Gabe dropped his controller in frustration, turning to look at Hunter. "We don't have a bird."

When they went down for breakfast, Hunter looked over at the animal figurines his aunt had placed on the counter. They were all lined up, except, of course, the missing figure he took last night. That was when it occurred to him—that bird he saw last night looked an awful lot like the hawk figurine now stashed in his suitcase.

Could it be?

That night, when everyone was getting ready for bed, Hunter slipped down to the study and pocketed the remaining figurines. He quietly rushed back to his sleeping bag and stuffed them inside, near his feet.

He lay there for hours and hours to no avail. *What a stupid idea*, he thought before dozing off to sleep.

A loud crash from the hallway jolted him from his bed. *It's him*, Hunter thought. *The bird is back.*

Then a harsh roar came from the hallway, followed by a cacophony of screams and howls and hoots. Thundering paws clamored down the narrow passageway, ceramics and wooden statues breaking on the wood floors. The pounding of the paws grew louder, and Hunter jumped up, slamming the door just in time. Gabe finally came to.

"Quick! Throw my sleeping bag out the window," Hunter begged.

"What?" Gabe hadn't had time to process what was

happening. Bear claws the size of a kitchen knife pierced through the door. They only had a matter of seconds left.

"Just do it. Now!" Hunter pleaded.

Gabe crumpled up the heavy sleeping bag and opened the window, where the hawk that had haunted Hunter last night was hovering and pecking to get in. Gabe threw the bag straight at it, and the bag made a large thump as it landed on the ground two stories below. Instantly, all animal sounds of the night subsided.

Hunter and Gabe stared at each other, and they saw with disbelief that the giant punctures in the door had disappeared. The boys remained there until morning, neither able to fall back asleep, trying to put together what had just happened. They couldn't tell anyone. No one would believe them. Best to keep it to themselves.

"Boys, breakfast time!" a chirpy, kind voice called.

As Hunter went downstairs, he avoided his aunt's gaze. Had she noticed the figurines were missing? He pulled his hoodie down to cover his face.

As he sat at the table, instead of his morning cereal, he saw the animal figurines lined up on his placemat.

"I believe these are yours now," she said matter-of-factly, without meeting his gaze, while buttering her bread.

"Oh, I couldn't do that, Aunt Gigi. I don't have any money to pay you for them," Hunter mumbled.

"It's not about money, dear. You chose them, and in turn, they have chosen you. Look under their feet."

Hunter picked up the caribou, and sure enough, his initials were on the bottom.

"I made the same mistake. Envy comes for us all, I suppose. But now they're your burden to bear; that is, until the next unsuspecting greedy soul comes to your house."

"Look, I'm sorry, okay? I'm sorry. I've never taken anything before, and I won't do it again. Can't we just throw them out and call it even?"

"You can leave them behind, discard them, or drown them, but it won't matter. They will follow you. They will find their owner, and there is no escaping the night."

"So what do I do?" Hunter asked in desperation. "I can't live like this."

"I do recommend displaying them for all your friends to see." She chuckled. "And sleepovers might help."

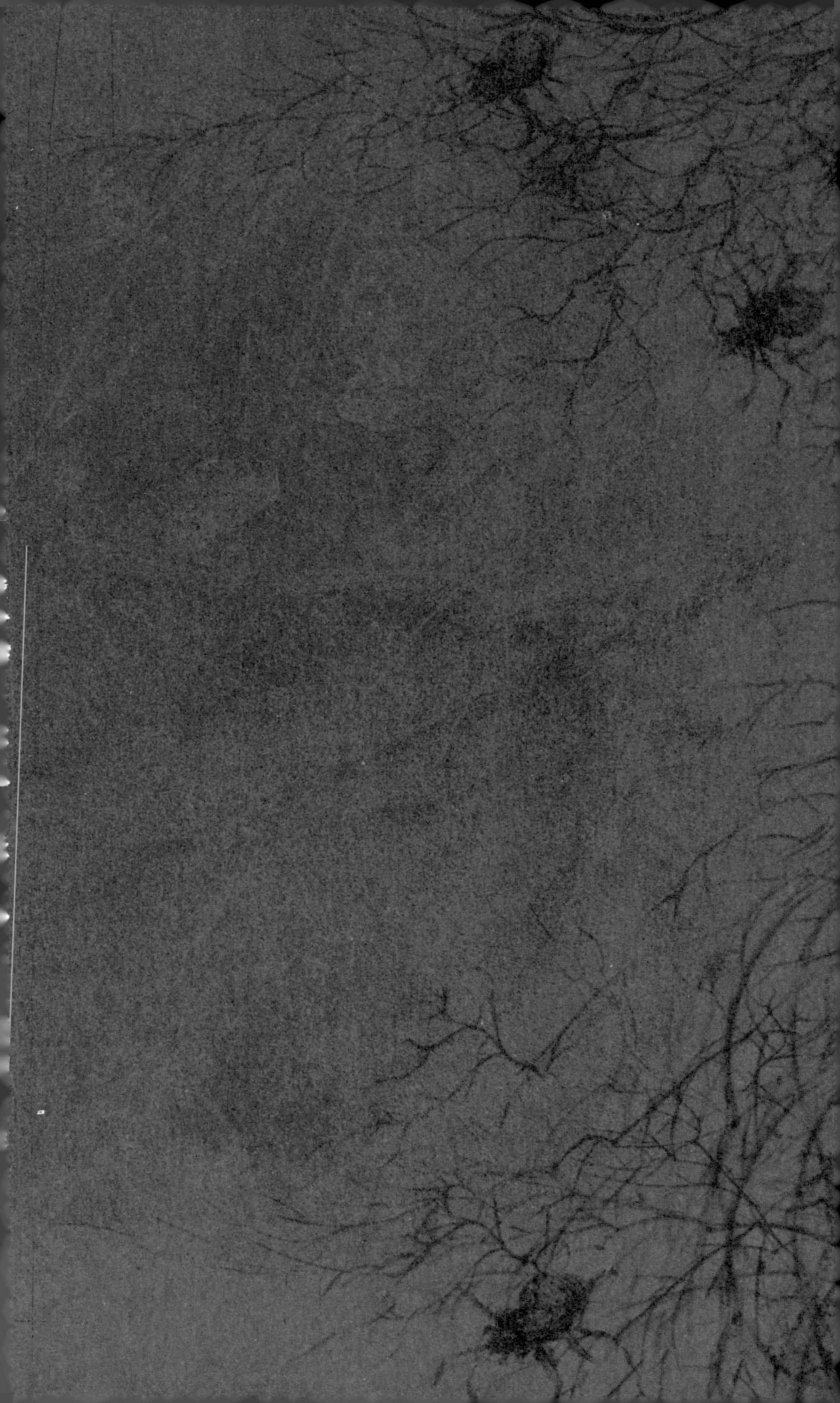

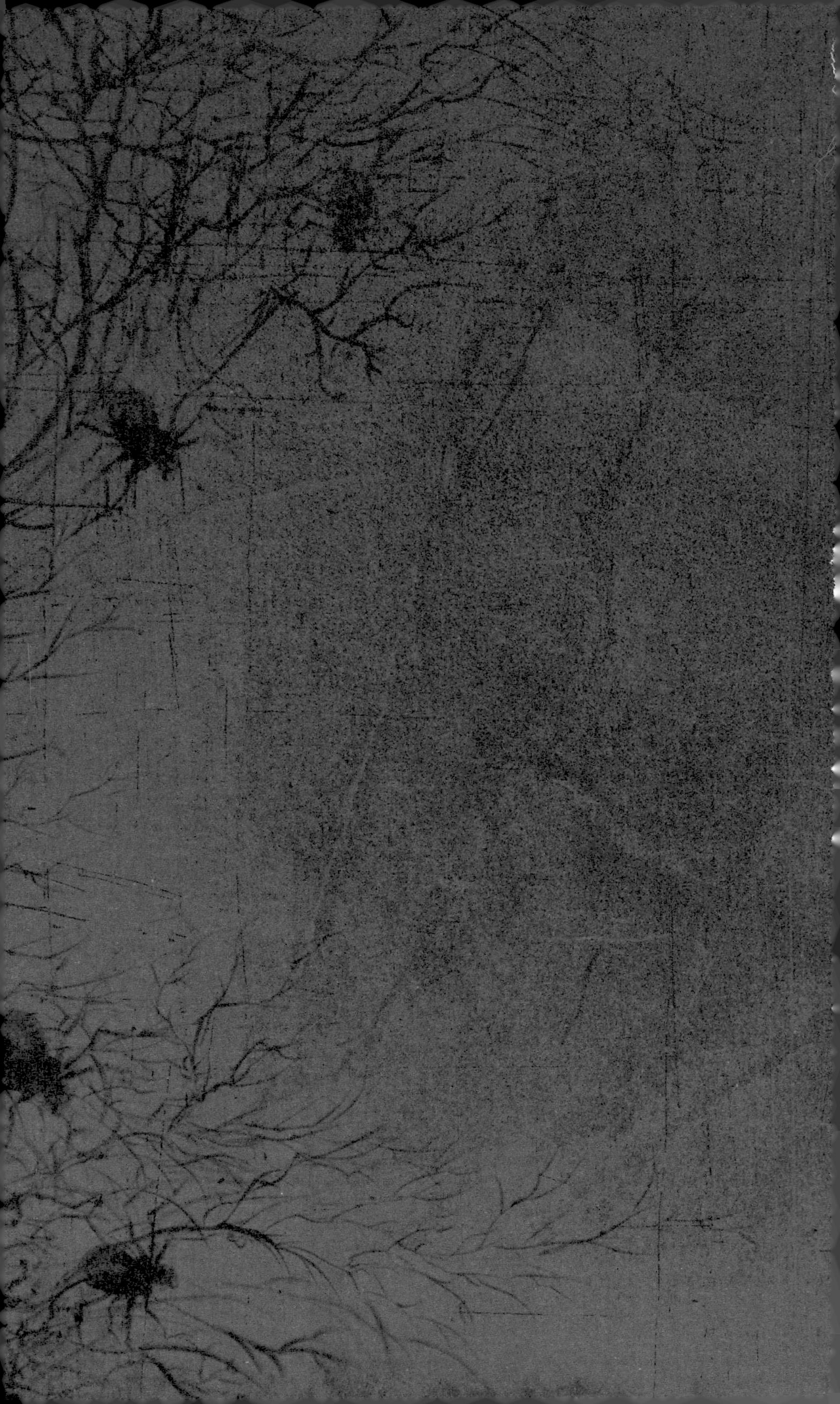